BISON
BOOKS

Books by Mari Sandoz
published by the University of Nebraska Press

The Battle of the Little Bighorn
The Beaver Men: Spearheads of Empire
The Buffalo Hunters: The Story of the Hide Men
Capital City
The Cattlemen: From the Rio Grande across the Far Marias
Cheyenne Autumn
Crazy Horse: The Strange Man of the Oglalas
The Christmas of the Phonograph Records
The Horsecatcher
Hostiles and Friendlies: Selected Short Writings of Mari Sandoz
Letters of Mari Sandoz
Love Song to the Plains
Miss Morissa: Doctor of the Gold Trail
Old Jules
Old Jules Country
Sandhill Sundays and Other Recollections
Slogum House
Son of the Gamblin' Man: The Youth of an Artist
The Story Catcher
These Were the Sioux
The Tom-Walker
Winter Thunder

THE *Story Catcher*

by

MARI SANDOZ

University of Nebraska Press
Lincoln and London

Manufactured in the United States of America

First Bison Book printing: 1986
Most recent printing indicated by the first digit below:
5 6 7 8 9 10

Library of Congress Cataloging in Publication Data
Sandoz, Mari, 1896–1966.
The story catcher.
"Bison."
Summary: A young Sioux warrior earns the right to be called historian for his tribe after numerous adventures and trials which test his ability to tell the story of his people with truth and courage.
[1. Dakota Indians—Fiction. 2. Indians of North America—Fiction]. I. Title.
[PZ7.S22St 1986] [Fic] 85-31810
ISBN 0-8032-9163-9 (pbk.)

Reprinted by arrangement with the Estate of Mari Sandoz, represented by McIntosh and Otis, Inc.

First published in 1963 by the Westminster Press

Dedicated to the Bad Heart Bull Family,
a long line of story catchers,
and particularly to Amos Bad Heart Bull,
artist and great historian of the Oglala Sioux.

Contents

1 / The Little Ree

YOUNG LANCE first noticed the small track in the fan of earth below a washout. He had slipped away from a scouting party with only his hunting bow, as one went for game, for meat. He had ridden his buckskin horse because the color was harder to detect in the fall breaks and gullies that he followed, trying to keep out of sight as much as possible as he watched the sky. Finally he saw what he sought, an eagle circling, very high up, like a wisp of soot from a campfire, floating on the wind. Over there must be the place, over where the eagle soared, the young Sioux thought, but because enemies might be watching, he held himself to caution and swung his horse far out around, to approach against the wind.

When he neared the spot, he got off and crept to the top of a low ridge. Head well down, eyes at the grass roots, he peered over into a little valley. There, on the wide creek bottoms below him, the eagle's shadow moved slowly over the yellowed grass, over the trampled place where the fight had been, with buzzards now quarreling at the dead horses, torn and dragged apart. Off to the side a big gray wolf was feeding at another carcass, alone and watchful, alert.

Suddenly the wolf leaped back, his nose lifted into the wind, his tail an erect plume. Then he was gone up a draw, the only sign of his passing the fall of a hovering magpie to the horse where the wolf had fed. But the big gray had not looked in the direction of Young Lance. His head had turned toward the low yellow line of brush along the creek. Unblinking, to miss not the slightest movement of a skulking enemy, the Indian youth held his eyes on the brush. He saw nothing except the passing shadow of the eagle still circling high above, and heard nothing more than the noisy squabble of the buzzards feeding where half a moon ago—two weeks by white man time—the hunters from his village had destroyed a small party of Rees trying to steal their horses. But the Sioux had lost a good man too, wounded here, to die on the way home. Now Young Lance had come to walk over the ground where this had been done, to think a little about the death of the man who had taught him and other youths to make good arrows, the iron points very sharp and secure, the feathers fastened carefully to balance the flight, each shaft painted with the owner's design.

Young Lance prepared carefully for his ride down the slope into the stink of the dead little battlefield, perhaps into an ambush. With a moccasin toe hooked over the back of the buckskin, one hand grasped into the black mane, the other with his bow and an arrow ready, he clung close to the side of the horse so that from far off there would seem to be no rider at all, and from near he would be hard to hit. As the horse plodded into the valley, the youth peered cautiously over the neck, trying to discover what had scared the hungry wolf away.

When he passed a group of dead horses where the Rees had made a stand, the buzzards lifted sullenly from their feeding, flew a short, awkward distance and settled along a cutbank to wait, their ugly naked heads bobbing in impatience. Lance found the spot where some men had fallen, and lay for a while, the marks of their bodies still plain, the earth darkened with their wounding. At least seven Rees were killed in the dawn attack that the Sioux scouts had discovered was coming, and turned into a trap. The returning party reported that they had cleaned out all the enemy they saw, but no one remained to search the weeds and brush after Arrow Man was found where he had been dropped by one of the first shots, struck in the throat.

The Ree bodies were all gone now, carried away for burial. Plainly the enemy knew of this place and might be watching to avenge themselves on any returning Sioux. Uneasy, Lance squinted his eyes carefully all around the ridges on both sides of the low valley and along the brush where something had scared the wolf. Seeing nothing to disturb the long-tailed magpies and the buzzards except himself, he began the search for the spot where Arrow Man fell and was carried away.

It was while the young Sioux rode back and forth examining the ground carefully that he saw the track in damp earth at the mouth of a washout—one fresh footprint, a little like a big raccoon's or a bear cub's, but not quite the same. The toes were short and stubby, without claws—the bare foot track of a man-being, small but certain, and very fresh, the track of an enemy here, now.

At this realization Lance slid down the far side of his horse again for protection from arrow or lead ball. He peered cautiously through the black mane of his horse, afraid that hesitation might bring an attack, afraid too that any move might take him straight into an ambush, with only his hunting bow, and all alone. Nobody knew where he was. None would carry him away, wounded as Arrow Man had been, or even find his body except by watching the eagles and the buzzards flying.

To fool at least a far observer he guided his horse to wander in a sort of aimlessness, grabbing a mouthful of grass here and there on the way to a deep gully, up which one might escape if attack came. Then Lance saw something creep from the brush of the bottoms into a clump of russet slough grass. It was a naked Indian, but very small, either dwarfed or a child that seemed not over four years old, and grasping a knife that caught one ray of the sun and was lost. The little Indian kept hidden only a moment before he peered from the tall growth and began to crawl again, from clump to clump, afraid but coming closer.

Something about the movement, so like a shy but curious young creature, a fawn or a cub, made Lance less cautious. The small one seemed such a wildling too, a lostling, alone. Gently the youth urged his horse around, but the little Indian, suddenly alarmed, rose and ran stooping back into the brush and was gone with scarcely a tremble of a browning leaf to show his hiding place.

For a long time Lance watched the autumn rosebushes, until he remembered that there must be other Indians around. Swiftly he glanced over all the death-smelling little valley and back to where the small boy had flattened down like a young quail taking on the color of the growth around it. In the quietness the buzzards stalked back to their angry feeding, and finally the small Indian, too, seemed to lose his fear.

The bushes shook a little, a reddened leaf fell, and an eye peered out, staring and plain. It was so funny that for a moment Lance forgot the danger and forgot that he was a budding young warrior before an enemy. He laughed aloud, slipped from his horse and dove for the boy, who slashed out with his knife and scurried away, dodging back and forth, quick as a little fox in the long grass. Finally, Lance had the naked body about the waist, and grabbing the boy's hand, made him let go of the knife. The Sioux got a good raking of fingernails down his cheek, but with the small hands tied behind the boy's twisting back with a rawhide thong, Lance squatted down and smiled into the furious, frightened little face. Slowly he spoke the Sioux word for Ree, and made the corn-shelling motion with the hands that was the sign for the tribe. Then he added the sign for friendship, his hand raised, palm out—the left one because it was nearest the heart and had shed no man's blood.

The boy stared at him, and Lance tried more signs, asking where the others were, his mother, his father. The little Ree stood unmoving as a rock, his face stony too, until Lance reached into the skin pouch at his belt and brought out a chunk of pemmican, of *wasna.* Then the boy jerked his tied arms around to grab for the meat. One of the hands was freed and as the boy gnawed at a corner of the stone-hard *wasna* with his sharp teeth, Lance realized how starved the scrawny little body was, the brown arms and legs thin as willow sticks.

"You *are* a lost one!" he exclaimed.

The voice if not the words seemed to make the boy realize his helplessness. He stopped his chewing, the *wasna* in his hands forgotten as he pulled into himself, shrank together as a frightened bird caught in closing fingers.

When the sun began to settle behind the ridge where a wolf came to wait and two coyotes slunk in and out of a draw, Lance decided it might be safe to start back through the shadowing slopes and breaks. He tied a rawhide string around the boy's middle, fastened the end to his own elbow and lifted the light little body to ride behind him on the buckskin. He had hoped to sneak in through the darkness without facing questions from Jumping Moose, the scout leader, about where he had been, but that was impossible now. Even Arrow Man, the one he had come to mourn, seemed forgotten under the song Young Lance found himself humming to the gentle lope of his horse until he felt the boy behind him slyly working at the knot in the rawhide string that held him. He turned and managed to grab the little Ree before he could slip off, hide in the tall, shadowed grass. With the boy swung around before him, and set hard across the horse, to be held firmly there, Lance realized he would have to watch this brave and designing little captive very carefully for a long, long time. And what about the mourning relatives of Arrow Man? Would they welcome an enemy Ree into the village now, even this small one?

Lance thought about these things as night crept out of the canyons. "Your name—perhaps it will be Arrow Boy, for the man killed there, but everybody will call you the little Ree, or even Little Left Behind one. You will be one more small Sioux at our fire, to sit beside my little blood brother, Laughing Cub—a sort of twin with him, like my twin sisters—"

Lance said this in Sioux, and the little Ree would not have understood if he had heard. By now he was heavy on the arm of his captor, sleeping in the warmth of a robe for the first time in the cold nights of October, of the Moon of Falling Leaves. So the two rode into the scout camp, the boy scarcely waking when Lance handed him down to the men gathered around. They had risen angrily from their hidden evening coals to demand an explanation from the youth they had taken along only to please his father. Now they stood around the boy, talking back and forth over his drooping head, letting Young Lance know that his sneaking away was not to be overlooked. It might have brought an arrow to his heart and even now was endangering the whole scout camp by alerting the enemy to their presence. Then for the time of a star's fall they showed elation over the enemy caught, a young Ree who might be made into a good Sioux if what Lance said about him proved straight and true—a very resourceful and strong Sioux, even though he was scarcely big enough for his first rabbit bow.

But the kind of man he became, and whatever his presence among them brought upon the people would be the responsibility of his captor, Jumping Moose, the young war chief of the seven scouts here reminded Lance. "We will hold you for any bad thing he does. You gave him life when you should have killed him, killed your first enemy to bring honor to your mother and your sisters in the ceremonial dancing. You denied them this honor, this pride, and lost the avenging of Arrow Man, your second uncle."

Jumping Moose said this so fiercely that the small Ree awoke. Seeing all the men tall about him in the night, he clutched at Lance for protection and in the comforting, the young Sioux felt a warmth run through his arms, and a hardening determination as he stooped to shelter the thin, shaking little body.

"I will make him a Sioux, and my relatives will dance his coming, dance it in joy," Lance replied. It was a bold speech, as the young Indian knew, remembering that his mother was wearing ashes in her hair, and gashes on her arms for the death of Arrow Man by the Rees.

The two were hastily fed a little roasted meat, the boy half asleep yet still afraid, looking around the dark, light-touched faces of his enemies as he chewed until his eyes fell shut and his jaws stopped. By then the horses had been brought in, quietly but swiftly, and the camp began to move, one rider after another disappearing into the darkness. The little bed of fire coals was ringed with upturned sod to prevent a spread into the dry prairie, but left glowing for a long while after everyone was far away. The Rees would make a rescue attack as soon as they knew the boy was alive, certainly as soon as scouts or mourners found tracks at the fighting ground. There might even be a big pipe-carrying to the other tribes, particularly the Pawnees, to raise a great war march against the Sioux, one that could wipe out this insult.

Jumping Moose headed his party of scouts southwestward in the clouding night. Young Lance carried the sleeping little captive before him, holding him safe but without triumph now. He realized that the sudden breakup of the scouting was his fault and that whatever came of this failure to watch for enemy war parties would be upon him. He rode in the middle of the single file, the place for any who could not be trusted, any who must be watched. Several times Lance looked back into the blackness that lay over the ancient country of the Rees, the Arikaras, who carried many old angers against the Sioux, and now had these new ones.

Jumping Moose camped his party through the daylight time in broken country, hiding so no enemy scouts could see their retreat from the borders of their hunting grounds, know that they were no longer out guarding. There were some angry eyes turned toward the little Ree, and Young Lance realized that an enemy glimpse of the boy would bring an attack, perhaps an overwhelming attack, upon their small party here, eight men counting himself if his arm could prove a man's in a fight. So they must keep hidden, and a relay of watchers out while the rest of the party slept a little. Lance had tied the Ree to his left arm, the knots next to his ribs where a touch would bring a tickling. Worn as the boy must be, Lance felt him lying awake, holding himself still, and so the young Sioux loosened the rawhide thongs and began to whisper friendly sounds to the little captive. The boy stared at him with eyes as unmoving as the black glass from which the old ones had made knives—without warmth, only the cold hardness of courage.

After a while Lance sat up and smoothed the dust before him. With a weed stalk he drew the picture of a lean, fox-faced boy, the eyes big and round, the pupils ringed out to show them staring. As Lance worked, the little Ree watched, squatting and silent, until suddenly a small laugh escaped him, but he clapped a thin hand over his mouth, his eyes still the smoky dark of an enemy.

Lance pulled out the piece of *wasna* left in his belt pouch, laid it on a rock and struck it with his knife blade, cutting it into two parts. He motioned with the point toward one of the pieces. The boy reached for it, but cautiously, as though afraid of an equal blow from the knife. Lance pretended he did not see this fear. Instead, he made the offering of his piece toward the sky, the earth, and the four directions, and began to gnaw at it. So they ate together, but the boy seemed to stiffen once more, perhaps remembering. To make the Ree laugh again, Lance made a picture of a small Indian chasing a rabbit that popped into a hole, and of another one sneaking a piece of meat from the drying racks, and a woman after him with a burning stick from the fire. He drew a horse race, the winner a boy sticking on like a wildcat, with all four feet and hands, the scrubby little pony running with his belly almost to the ground, his long, straggly tail sticking straight out, all the other horses in the whirl of dust far behind.

Slowly the little Ree put out a finger and drew the figure of a boy, just straight lines for the body, the legs and arms, and a circle on top for the head, with braids. It was a riding boy, riding behind a stick man on a running horse drawn the same way. Then he made another picture, of a woman, lines too, but with a skirt, a woman standing all alone. A moment the small boy looked down upon his pictures and then threw himself over them, sobbing silently.

So Lance was caught trying to slip away the second time on this one scouting trip, this time to get the little Ree to his people if he could. But the guards brought him back, and Jumping Moose stood up to his full tallness in his robe. "You are a leaky kettle in which to cook the soup of responsibility!" he roared, in the voice that could tame the most arrogant young warrior.

Then, remembering that an enemy might hear, he made the gesture for striking, and suddenly Lance faced his first public punishment, public humiliation, knowing in that swift moment a thankfulness that Blue Dawn was not there to see, with pain or scorn in her pretty young eyes. Nor would his parents have to see this, or his sisters. But mostly he was thankful about Dawn and his only brother, the small one called Laughing Cub.

By now two of the guards had stepped up with their bows and whipped Lance across the shoulders, each man striking twice, for the number of foolish acts. The shamed youth braced himself against the blows and kept his lean face as stony as the little Ree's had been, but as the striking continued, the boy cried out, and breaking from the man who held him, he ran under the upraised bow and clutched Young Lance about the knees.

That evening they moved out in the first darkness. The Ree was not with Lance this time. Instead, he was on the horse of a more trustworthy one, a man. When they reached home there was no triumphant singing into the village, only a silent signaling from the guards and a quiet taking to the council lodge to explain the sudden and dangerous return of a scouting party before another had gone out to take its place. No one spoke to Young Lance, not even a blaming word or a look of the eye, not from his friends, suddenly as shy-faced as the few girls who saw them, or from his father, Good Axe, seated among the council with the pipe. If there was talk about the Ree captive, it was in the quiet words at the back of the council, with old Sun Shield as always in the honored place, and Good Axe and the rest of the headmen. The little Ree, asleep by now, was carried away to a warrior lodge, as was proper with a captive. Lance did not dare to look up then or when they left the council, but he was certain Dawn was not among those standing to look toward them from the fire where they were dancing.

At his home lodge his mother made no greeting to be passed to him through a third person, as any word must be between a mother and her blood son after his seventh year. There were friends and other relatives in the big warm lodge, but the firelight and the soft murmur of talk washed around Lance like creek water around a stone. No one mentioned the enemy Ree brought here among them, although the mother's mourning garments were not yet discarded. Lance could not even be certain that anyone had spoken to her of his sneaking away or of his captive, through whom he had endangered the scouts and all his village as no one, not even a newborn child, must ever be permitted to do.

There were no words from his father or even his second parents, and nothing of what would be done about the enemy boy in the camp that still mourned a good man killed by one of the Rees.

Lance did not sleep in the lodge of either mother but went to one of the wickiups of his cousins. He waited until the others seemed asleep and then crept into the robes as silently as possible. He lay a long time scarcely breathing, afraid someone had heard him, afraid someone might speak. Afterward he just stared into the darkness of the low shelter, wondering who had the frightened little Ree now, and what would happen when the widow of Arrow Man saw the boy.

2 / The Pit and the Surround

YOUNG LANCE awoke from an uneasy night dream in which the Little Ree was being stolen, the village attacked. He lifted his head and found himself still in the low wickiup, his cousins gone, and a sound of horses running outside. But from behind him came a man's voice singing to welcome the sun for a good day.

Lance lifted the flap of the shelter and looked out, his braids shaggy from three days without the quill combing, his face lean and uneasy in the morning light. There was commotion among the pointed skin lodges of Sun Shield's village, the old crier running around the large circle, drumming and shouting something. The women looked up from their cooking fires where the smoke rose blue to spread against the reddened sky, and then bent to their work again.

Lance could see almost no young people around, not his friends Deer Foot and Cedar nor the girls like Dawn and her companion Shying Leaf. Small boys ran here and there, gathering like young antelope at play. Lance shaded his eyes against the sun just topping the eastern hills, and looked for the little Ree, but he was not out anywhere; yet the hurry in the village was not against an enemy. There were no gatherings at the lodges of the warrior societies, and no one was painted for a fight. Even the horses whooped in from the hills were not war chargers but mostly the pack and drag mares and the fast buffalo runners. It must be a hunt camp going out. At such a time, Lance knew, anyone in disgrace must not push forward. The buffaloes came in plenty only when everything was well done, the women pure, the men honorable and brave.

The young Sioux slipped out of the wickiup and around the village to the river. He broke the thin fringing of bank ice, washed some of the weariness from his face and re-braided his hair so he could appear decently for his morning meal. He went to the fire of Feather Woman, who had been selected as his second mother when he was born, as was proper. The second mother could scold the son directly or praise him and show affection in a way that would keep a blood son an infant tied to the mother's moccasin heels all his life.

Feather looked up as Young Lance approached, coming quietly and in deference. "You are late, my son," she said. "One cannot sleep the troubles away."

She said this half in blaming but in a warm and teasing voice, and when she saw the shame in the youth's face, she laughed a little. "It can all pass with the falling leaves," she added, and selected one of the young ducks roasting around a bed of coals. "Eat," she said, handing him the cool end of the roasting stick. "The others are gone ahead. Buffaloes have been seen."

Ah-h, that was good.

"It has been decided that you are to stay here, with those who care for the village, with the old and the sick."

Lance did not lift his head, apparently staring at the duck on the end of the smooth stick. "The little Ree?" he dared ask at last.

"We will take him. The warriors will be at the hunting and can fight off anyone coming for him. Pawnee Woman, who speaks Ree, discovered that the boy is the son of the war chief killed. He was left behind, out of the fight, and none lived to go to him. So he wandered and found the place from the buzzards flying."

Lance moved uneasily. "I know it was dangerous to bring him here."

"Yes, very dangerous when the Rees discover that he still lives."

Lance did not reply, and the woman busied herself and did not make him shamefaced, bad-faced, by comfort offered as to a boy, not to one entering his warrior years. After a while Lance remembered the roasting stick in his hand, the weight and smell of the duck on it. He pulled off a brown, juicy leg but held it untasted. "We shall try to be good sons to you, my mother, and to all the village," he promised, but he spoke the words very low, and without confidence.

Young Lance knew that the long snows of winter and spring would cut deep into the fattest parfleches of dried meat and *wasna.* Those in the village of Sun Shield were still less than half full, buffaloes were scarce, and the big fall hunt was yet to be made. A blizzard might strike any day and scatter the herds into little bunches for all the winter, make them wild and hard to find, and leave the stomachs in the lodges very, very thin before the grass returned. True, the hunters would push out into the worst cold to find a deer or an elk, never more than a good smell on the wind to a hungry village.

There should be new robes too, heavy-furred for the lodge floors, warm beds, and to wear against the blizzard winds. There should be fine hides worth the art of the special robe workers among the women—his mother and the others—hides to be chipped thin on the inside for lightness and tanned almost as soft as deerskin—fall hides, the wool dark and glossy in the firelight. During the long days when the cottonwoods popped from the freezing cold the women would adorn the best robes with paint and beading for the headmen, the very finest of all to be offered in the thanking ceremony to the buffalo.

Today the great fall hunt was to start, and glory might come to some young hunter among those selected to do the killing. Lance could have been among them but now he would not even help with the butchering. He knew there were some who thought just taking the little Ree along would bring bad luck, and besides, there was no telling what might be done to the boy if the Rees attacked and another Sioux was lost to their arrows, their guns. Someone, man or woman, wild with grief, might make the heart good again by killing this handy enemy, even if only a small boy. Then what would Young Lance and his warrior relatives do? He had brought the Ree boy into the village as his captive, his chosen brother.

Lance had thought about some of these things when he had heard fresh scouts go out last night to watch where his party should have stayed. Jumping Moose and his men weren't among them or even among the hunters. They would stay to guard the village here, the lodges, goods and horse herds, and to protect those unable to follow the hunt—the old, the crippled and sick. Some of the strong women were also staying, perhaps with very new babies in the cradleboards, and some to help prepare for the meat and robes to come. All the rest except Lance went, the little Ree too, riding in a pony drag with several other children.

Young Lance watched the hunt camp move out into the early fall sun, following the path of the shooters who had gone ahead yesterday and in the night. The people made a long line, with warriors far ahead and around the sides.

Most of the young women and girls rode together, Dawn and her friends among them, their eyes surely glancing out toward the young men protecting the marching camp. The center was mostly the families, with a few young men there too, to help. Many of the women and older men had pony drags behind their horses, some with the butchering things, a few with small tipis for the night, and others with willow cages to keep the children and loose articles from falling out. The small Ree looked back from one of these, but only at first. Soon the excitement of the moving people made him forget the young Sioux who had given him the sign for "friend" out on the place of the fight.

When the dust of the last drag pole had spread against the bluffs, Lance felt he could not endure the quietness of the village or the eyes of the widow of Arrow Man turned politely from him so there could be no public blaming. Forgetting the danger of attack from Ree, or from Pawnee or Crow, with the hunters gone, Lance wandered off. Once he tossed a bone at the scavenging magpies that helped keep the campground clean, and watched them fly up, trailing their long tails. Beyond them he noticed an eagle circling slowly, dipping, only to rise again, soaring on the wind, his sharp eyes hunting for rabbit or for some fresh carcass—hungry too—in the scarcity of remains from buffalo hunts.

Looking back to watch the eagle circling a little, Lance ran to his lodge. There he threw his small buffalo robe over his shoulder and gathered up his bow and an old piece of deerskin. No one tried to stop him as he started away afoot to climb the steep slope from the creek to the fall-yellowed plain spreading away northward. Out of sight from the village he circled back to where the tableland broke into a high limestone butte called the Lookout. There he squatted in his robe and scowled off to the dark scattering of the horse herds on the far open prairie where the approach of enemies could be seen, and then down to the smoky lodges of his village. He could see the figures of women out along the creek bottoms, looking as short as children from so far. He knew some were filling their robes with sweetgrass and herbs to line the parfleche cases for the dried meat from the hunt. He could hear the far thump of hatchets where some chopped up old travois poles or cut down bunch willows to build the meat racks and hide stretchers needed if the hunt was good.

The youth knew how it would be out with the buffalo surround, the excitement of it, with his little Ree brother there and the rest of his family and his friends too. Only he was missing, not even there to help finish off any down animal that came suddenly alive and charged the butchering ones. Instead, he was up here, on Lookout, wishing he had a clean hide or a smooth piece of wood for the pictures always in his mind, even here, where he had come to search out an old, old eagle pit. By the time he found it, half full of trash and sand and fallen willow poles, a second eagle had joined the hunting one, both high up, two bits of black moving against the whitish sky.

Lance slid out of sight into the old pit and began to dig at the trash, piling everything carefully upon his robe, to be carried far away without leaving a sign of man anywhere. When he was down to rock, he replaced the thin screening of willows over the hole, using the old rotten ones to cover the solid new poles he brought from the bottoms. With the place looking as undisturbed as before, he shot a rabbit and tied the carcass firmly to the top of the willow covering, the side of the animal opened red to the sky. Then, although the eagles were gone and he was cold and hungry, Lance crawled under the willow cover to the pit to wait.

It was warm out of the wind, and when he began to doze a little he threw off the robe to recapture the sharp alertness of cold, his eyes watching the pale sky, the piece of deerskin ready. Toward evening an eagle appeared out of the south, flying fast. He circled nearer, spiraling lower and lower. Suddenly the wings folded, and the eagle struck like an arrow upon his prey, sinking his talons into the rabbit, the great wings flapping out to rise, the whole pit cover rocking. Young Lance grabbed through the willows for the powerful legs, caught one, and then the other, the eagle pounding his wings harder and driving his angry beak at the wood that seemed to hold him. The knife-sharp talons slashed sideways at the youth's wrists so the blood ran, the pain burned, but he clung to the legs and tried to grasp both of them in one hand so he could work the deerskin over the clawing feet to protect his arms. He had to keep his head bowed to protect his eyes, his shoulders hunched against the sharp tearing beak and the thrashing wings as the willows flew apart in the fierceness of the eagle's fury. The powerful bird struck again and again upon the unprotected head and shoulders, his beak cutting and ripping the flesh of the arm thrown up to shield the youth's eyes, the wings like war clubs upon him. But Lance hung on, and at last his right hand, slippery with blood, clutched the sinewed, pulsating throat, and his thumb shut off the windpipe. Panting open-beaked, the eagle struggled in one last burst of power and then began to weaken. Finally the great wings settled, dark and protective, around the dying bird and the young hunter.

It was sunset before Lance had the strength to climb out of the pit and start home. His cut and torn head and face, his hands and arms were bloody and sand-caked, his swollen shoulders painful under the weight of his first eagle, the great eagle of the golden head.

Two old men ran out of the village to meet the young Sioux. They spread the wings of the eagle between them, exclaiming at the breadth from tip to tip, reaching farther than the length of a man, the bloody flesh of the hunter speaking of a battle that would bear recounting for many moons, the scars of his shoulders to last longer. It was a solemn thing that this Young Lance who was not permitted to go with the hunt today should take an eagle in the old pit, without a vision, a medicine guidance, a leader, or anyone to tell him how it was done.

But now the young eagle catcher must be taken to the creek to bathe in the cold, cleansing water and then be fed. Unfortunately his father was not there to sing the deed through the village, but the news spread and everybody ran out to see the eagle catcher brought in. Although the widow of Arrow Man did not ask him to her lodge to eat, she sent a bighorn spoon full of soup with a large chunk of tender venison and a lot of wild turnip and onion in it. It was a man's meal, and Lance managed it all, until he was stuffed like a badger for hibernation. But better than the food was the generous way of the woman whose husband had been lost to the Rees.

When Lance rose from his sleep the next morning he found a new deerskin breechclout laid at the lodge door by someone. He unfolded the long flaps, gay with beads, their pattern not from any design he could recognize, perhaps made by Pawnee Woman, a long-time captive among them, a cousin to the Rees. Anyway, the gift helped relieve some of the soreness in his whole body, but there was nothing more done about the eagle. The hunt camp returned, too soon and silently, without song or messenger ahead to shout the news of a great feast. They had obtained very little meat and a few robes. The buffaloes were wild and scattered from a recent hunting party, Pawnee, it seemed; at least, the arrows in the fresh and bleeding wounds of some fat cows were Pawnee marked.

Jumping Moose examined the shafts brought in. "I think the hunters may have been Rees, using some arrows of the Pawnees."

Yes, the scouts had signaled a large Ree trail coming north and had picked up stories from the wind. The little tribe was moving back up to the Missouri, deserting their village ground near the rock that the whites called the Chimney and all the country of their Pawnee relatives.

Young Lance heard this with concern. If any of them passed the place of the fight, with the tracks still fresh, undimmed by rain or snow, surely some would come searching for the little left behind one.

Sun Shield's village was silent and dark very early that night, without one word about the torn face and hands of Young Lance, not even from his mother or the twin sisters or from Deer Foot and Cedar—not one compassionate glance from Blue Dawn. Instead, it seemed he was blamed for the bad buffalo hunt. Perhaps he should have saved the eagle and hung him ostentatiously on a pole at the lodge door, but he had skinned the bird very carefully, saving the wings for fans, one for his father, Good Axe, the other for Moccasin, the second father that every young Sioux must have. Luckily, eagles had two wings, so he did not need to choose between the men. The tail feathers were for the hair and toward a warbonnet for someone, someday—particularly those with the fluffy whiteness called breath feathers. The body skin he would tan for his hunting shirt, for the power he hoped it would bring to his striking arm, power and with it the sharp, far-seeing eye of the eagle.

The next morning Lance sat out on a bank above the wickiups, drawing pictures in the sand for the little Ree, teaching him the Sioux words for such things as meat, buffalo, horse, and man. He added other words too that any boy must know: "hungry," "sleepy," "hurt," and "cold" and "I did this," "I did not do that." Lance started to add the statement, "It is true," one not necessary for a Sioux, it was fondly believed, but enemies sometimes spoke with a forked tongue. Lance laughed a little at the idea, and the boy echoed him, not understanding but needing to agree, his dark eyes lifted to his captor's. Immediately he was serious again, his stare unblinking as he began to form more of the new words: "I should like—" and then added the common signs for "go" and "home."

"No!" Lance said sternly. "You cannot go home," grabbing the boy's arms and pressing them to his sides to emphasize his captivity. The little Ree stood motionless between the restraining hands, as stony and furious as the day he was caught. Yet today the ribs were less sharp under the new doeskin shirt, and there was a softening about the boy, a softening from warmth and people, a cozy sleeping space at the lodge fire of Good Axe, and warm soup in the horn spoon.

Slowly the youth released the thin arms and had to see the hands move defiantly into more signs: "My people, they will come!" The whole small body defiant, afraid, with enemies all around here, and yet so defiant.

Before the horses and the hunting equipment were put away new buffalo ceremonials were begun, with more than the usual concentration, and a little desperation too, because the blizzard time was so near. The older men worked with pipe and story and sacred objects in the rites for meat, and afterward some of them escorted the buffalo scouts on their way. In the meantime the youths were testing their prowess with bow and arrow and big talk while the hunters sharpened the knives again and the iron points of the arrows and the spears, so sharp that a good spear man could bring a buffalo bull to his knees with one proper thrust under the shoulder blade.

Young Lance was out with the horse guards. He had wanted to take the little Ree along, but Jumping Moose motioned the boy back to the family lodge to play with

Laughing Cub. "Too dangerous with the herds," the man said. The horse raiders always sneaking around might see him.

Lance knew that this was true, and so he hunted up a bleached buffalo head and with a piece of charcoal drew a picture of the horses running together, heads over each other's necks. Someday he would show it to the little Ree, when it was safer to bring him up here.

That evening Lance discovered that he had been selected, with Deer Foot and Cedar, to help the warrior society police the coming buffalo hunt. Although he had brought an enemy among the mourners, it was decided that his medicine was very strong, to catch a great eagle. He was the youngest of all the village to catch one with the hands, and the only one who did this alone, without adviser or trainer. Perhaps such medicine could help toll the buffaloes as it had drawn the eagle out of the wide, wide sky.

Lance helped with the family horses and weapons, and was half promised the use of his father's gray hunting horse, old and reliable, and his buffalo bow, very strong, but now perhaps he could pull it, at least a few times. Anyway, he had his own bow with which he had killed two yearlings in the summer hunt. True, the wool was thin then, but who could say what power the bow might have now?

After these announcements in the village circle Lance felt better than any time since Arrow Man's body was carried to the burial tree. He joined the other youths along the evening path from the river for a glimpse, even a gay word if one were bold, with the girls as they passed carrying the waterskins. He tried to take Cub and the Ree along there too, but his father thought it was better to wait until the moon of mourning was past. Lance's twin sisters were there, carrying their small waterskins—pretty girls, with shy but wandering eyes, already managing to be noticed by the watching youths, particularly Dancer, a thin, swift-legged boy of thirteen whose dream was to be a great runner. Cedar and Deer Foot were with Lance and made soft teasing words for Dawn and Shying Leaf and the rest.

On the third day, toward evening, the scouts signaled the sight of a great buffalo herd one half day's travel west. The men did not come in for the usual feast and ceremonies. Great white owls were seen in the treetops, which meant a deep-snow winter, and coming very soon. Besides, the scouts must watch the moving herd, keep it together with careful use of the man-smell, and fight off any enemies come to shoot for meat.

Because it seemed they might need the power and boldness of the eagle, Lance put on the shirt with the eagle-skin back and was ready early. The planners among the hunters were gone before dawn, and a little later the old crier ran through the village calling to those who were to follow. "Get ready to move, my friends! Go swiftly but carefully, in the good way, and we shall make plenty of meat!"

Some members of the policing society went early, ten abreast, to guard against anyone trying to sneak out for a shot ahead of the surround, which would surely scare the herd and spoil the hunt. Such reckless ones were to be knocked off their horses. Behind the first warriors the main body of hunters rode out, in rows of five, and then the people strung along far over the prairie with their travois and pack horses. While they moved, the head men selected a few of the best hunters with the fastest horses. "Young warriors, brave relatives," they sang. "You have good bows. Everything you do is good, so today you are to shoot to feed the helpless, the old, those without strong sons, and those with no man left. Everything you kill shall be theirs."

Lance was back among the youths guarding the sides of the moving camp as the selected hunters came together in a little line and the women and girls lifted their voices in a trilling of praise. At the last stop the hunters got ready for the kill while the people stayed behind, out of sight and downwind so no man-smell would reach the half-blind, sharp-nosed buffaloes. The women unpacked and put up the small tipis. Some cut willows for meat racks here if the hunt should be a good one.

In the meantime Lance and other young hunters, with Moccasin to control their excitement, rode down a draw into the wind. As they came out on a wide valley they heard a rising thunder of hoofs and saw a large herd begin to run together as the first of the surround men charged from their scattered hidings. They struck the buffaloes obliquely all around and started the herd into a loose circular run. Here and there the sun flashed on an iron point. Perhaps a buffalo went down, then more, the hunters crying their "Yihoo!"

"Go!" Moccasin motioned, and the youths whipped in, one behind the other, Lance with his father's long bow, all heading for the yearlings and other younger animals. Deer Foot brought one down and shouted his triumph. Then a shaggy, panting old bull dropped out of the herd, dodged behind a hunter and before the man could turn his wild, excited horse and bring down the worthless bull that might start a break in the circling, the animal charged Lance's gray horse with his clumsy, woolly head. With no time to dodge, the horse went down and Lance, both hands on the long bow, was thrown over the gray's head upon the staggering buffalo, the bow knocked free into the dust. For a moment Lance got a hand in the hump wool and then he leaped to the ground and ran, several fat cows thundering past him, his horse up and after them, as any good buffalo horse should. Then the herd was gone and Lance was among the dark carcasses.

He whistled, saw the gray stop, come back, and so he rode to find the big bow. It was in the trampled earth, but somehow unbroken. To make certain that it would be safe he took it to a sandy knoll, stuck it upright into the ground and then charged on to the still circling herd. Up beside the galloping animals, he fired one arrow after another from his small bow. The first brought a cow staggering to her knees, bleeding from the nose, but Lance was already after another, sinking arrows into a young spike-horned bull, and then a second cow, his shouts of triumph lost in the thunder and yells over the wide valley.

With his quiver empty, Lance turned back to locate his kills. "Here!" Moccasin called, waving. Deer Foot and Cedar rode in too, and seven others, searching among the down animals, picking out their buffaloes by the arrow patterns. The young hunters had eleven among them, some not quite dead, one shot with the arrows of two. Three of the eleven buffaloes were Lance's.

By now the shooting was almost over, the thunder of hoofs far away, the hunters beginning to return on sweating, dusty horses. The valley was dotted with the black carcasses, a scattering stretched out for over a white man's mile on the path of the fleeing herd. It wasn't a close, compact kill, and would make much extra work for the butchers, for the women, but they came running in, trilling the happy meat song, their knives gleaming in the sun. Behind them ran the older ones, and the children, even the very small, while the hunters rode over the prairie to finish any buffalo still alive, perhaps to stagger to his feet and charge the helpless.

It was dusk before the butchering was done and the hides thrown, wool side down, over the pack horses, the meat piled on top, and the hanging ends folded neatly over the load. The leg bones were saved too, for the sweet, rich marrow, so good in soup or roasted, and, from the wiping fingers of the eaters, to make the braids shine. At the hunt camp big fires were built up to light the work while hump ribs roasted and spread their fine smell far over the prairie. The women stripped much of the meat into flakes thin as the edge of the hand for quick drying on the racks. Every now and then one or another stopped to sniff the far wind from the southeast, and blowing into snow.

Low fires were set under the meat racks and kept going all night. Early the next morning everything was loaded on travois and pack horses, and hurried homeward. Toward evening the sky darkened. Big snowflakes, like breast feathers from a swan, were falling by the time the pack horses of the men selected to shoot for those without hunters were tied to the proper lodges and met with songs of thankfulness. The rest of the meat was divided among those with someone in the hunt, except the fat young spike-horned bull that Lance shot. The horse bearing this meat he led to the widow of Arrow Man.

"It is the best one I killed," he managed to say, embarrassed and ashamed that it was not better.

The woman pushed back her loose mourning hair and tucked up her torn doeskin skirt. "I am thankful," she said, and busied herself unloading the meat, with Lance helping to ease the heavy hindquarters to the bed of silver sage spread on the ground.

At every lodge there was a hurrying to get everything under cover before the storm, already running in little white whirls through the village. The evening fires, perhaps the last outside for a long time, snapped and popped with fat buffalo ribs as the snow fell faster, until the coals were blackening under the storm. Then the meat was taken into the lodges, the finest to the leaders of the hunt, and to the warrior society that had policed the move and kept the overeager back so all could strike the circling herd. Afterward everybody slept, everybody except the guards at the horse herds and the scouts far out, huddling in their robes, out of the wind but alert, knowing that after a fat hunt the coyote and the Indian sleeps hard.

Most of the next day the lodges, each with a horse or two hunched together behind it, seemed only momentarily thicker whitenesses in the blizzard roaring so that not even a loud shout could be heard. Lance crept out with his robe about him to take his turn watching the horse herds. This was good raiding weather, and none to say who might be skulking around, Pawnee, Crow, or Ree. Later in the afternoon the sun broke through the clouds and sent long golden spears across the snow as Lance rode in to the lodge of Good Axe. He was drying himself at the fire beside Cub and the little Ree, who teased the twin sisters over on the woman's side of the lodge, when the crier came past.

"Lance! Young Lance, come to the council lodge!"

He went to stoop under the lodge flaps. Inside he saw the scout Running Elk stand before the hastily gathered council, telling about an enemy he killed just now. Returning from his post out in the storm he rode down between the wickiups and the lodges. His horse shied from a man skulking in the thinning snow, shied as from a stranger. The man started to run and fell over a picket rope, where Elk's stoneheaded war club ended him.

"The man had a long spear-knife and a ball pistol. He was a Ree."

"A Ree!" The angry exclamation ran around the circle of head men and the warriors standing behind them.

"How many more of the enemy have been permitted to reach the heart of a Sioux village?" old Sun Shield roared.

The scout dropped his head. No one could say, but a big party of warriors was already hurrying out to search the evening brush and breaks for other enemies, at least to find the man's horse. Jumping Moose had charged right out to the scout line.

"*Hou!*" It was good to know that some acted even after the enemy got into the village! Now there were other things to be done. Lance was sent to bring the little Ree, to discover if he knew the man. By then the first young warriors who had run in to strike the body, count coup on it, had been followed by many others, men, women, and younger ones come to stand, clutching their robes about them in the bitter cold, stony anger on many faces at this insult to the Sioux, the Plains' most powerful people. Even Arrow Man's widow came pushing through the crowd, her butcher knife out to strike the Ree, to avenge a good man's dying, but Sun Shield motioned her back.

"Your man deserved a better revenge, my sister," he said.

Pawnee Woman came and was led with Lance and the captive boy through the wall of Indians around the dead man still lying in the drifts. He was snow-caked and white, from heavy trader capote to moccasins, his upturned face calm as in sleep, with no blood showing anywhere. The Ree boy stared down at the man and then cried out a word that Pawnee Woman interpreted in a whisper: " 'Uncle,' he said, perhaps meaning any grown friend of the young—"

The boy did not seem to hear her. Confused, he looked up all around the circle of enemy Sioux standing in the bright evening snow, to the face of Lance. For him the boy made the sign of "gone under," dead, followed by the question sign. Lance bowed his head forward. Yes. Dead.

The captive boy drew his lips back in an angry snarl, his face that of an enraged warrior, but a very small one. Then suddenly he was a child, very much afraid among so many stern-eyed enemies. He grasped at the robe of his adopting brother, his face pressed hard into the snowy buffalo wool of it.

As the night settled, the half-faced moon climbed and grew brighter, but cold and far away above the frozen snow. The wolves started their howls along the ridges, and the coyotes too, thinner, higher, like wild women keening a wilder grief. Down in the village of Sun Shield a row of big brush piles blazed up to light all the wide camp and the dancing. First there had been a little victory ceremonial, made by Arrow Man's widow, washed and combed and in her best beading and fringe, now that the death of the Ree warrior had lifted her sad heart a little. She and her women relatives danced and sang the victory circle for Running Elk, who had avenged their grief. Later everybody went to the feasting and dances for the good hunt, the celebration of the big meat-making that was hastened but not reduced by the storm.

Lance went to stand at the dancing where the old woman of Dawn's home lodge watched, knowing that the girl was in the circle around that big fire somewhere. He pretended to have come just for the drumming and the songs but he joined quickly when he was called into the moving circle of dancers by one girl after another. Finally Dawn, too, held out her hand and he made the little running, bouncing steps with her on the frozen ground, the firelight reddening and heating the ring of young faces. It was the best time Lance could remember, but every little while he had to run back to make certain that the small Ree was safely sleeping beside Laughing Cub. One had to be very careful, with the Ree warrior killed not a far spear's throw from the fire of Good Axe.

When the moon settled into a clouding, the party of scouts was still away, looking for the enemies. It was difficult, with the tracks covered by the storm, and Lance grew more and more uneasy. Finally, he had to leave the dancing entirely, although Deer Foot was making his fancy little moccasin steps beside Dawn far too often.

From the lodge door Lance looked back to the ring of dark figures moving against the blazing fire and off toward the bluffs, a pale snow wall in the fading moon. Then he stooped under the skin flaps. The interior was dark; only one red eye of the lodge coals still gleamed. The youth slipped past the old woman resting near the opening, to see all who came and went. He glanced toward the back, where his father and mother slept in their robes, and settled beside his brothers to watch the night out. Even when his head drooped to his breast, the young Sioux was listening, up with his hand on his knife at the slightest crunch of frozen snow outside.

He would need more than the skin of the sharp-eyed eagle on his hunting shirt to see all the dangers ahead.

3 / Crow Butte

THE EARLY SNOW vanished almost as swiftly as it came, and was followed by a warm stillness that sent the ducks and geese, the turkeys and the swan, the beaver, the otter, the elk, and the buffalo all feeding hard. In Sun Shield's village the women hurried too, particularly with the robes. There were over a hundred fifty prime skins and not more than seventy good tanners, while in the bare trees the white winter owls still blinked and waited.

The girls helped with the meat under the direction of the older women. Lance's mother cared for both the robes and meat of the two buffaloes he brought home. She had made presents of choice pieces here and there, and by now the twins, Red and White Shell, almost twelve, could roast some of the jerked meat and then pound it with dried chokecherries and buffalo berries into a thick mixture. Crammed into dressed buffalo bladders and then dipped in hot tallow and hung away, this was the cherished pemmican, the *wasna*, the concentrated food to carry on hunt and scout and warpath.

Dawn and Shying Leaf and the other village maidens

were busy too, where all could see. It was true they must not be away from the eyes of the old women of their lodges, must avoid any suspicion of wrongdoing, for that would bring bad face to their families and scare the buffaloes away, the buffaloes that came only where the women were virtuous. Besides, it was a pleasure to see the shining young faces, the grace and gaiety of the maidens among them. Sometimes there were shy glances toward the youths who managed to have tasks that kept them around the meat and hide work, particularly the tall, lean Cedar, a trickster. He sneaked away two big bundles of the meat right under the hands of the girls, and stood laughing at their astonishment and confusion. Lance laughed too, farther off, making pictures of the hunt and the killing of the Ree warrior behind the lodges. He kept near his little captive brother, who looked upon the joking with sober, uncomprehending eye, as the stranger without the gift of the language must.

Three days later Young Lance and Deer Foot were out on the edge of the White Earth River breaks watching a small buffalo herd far off on the high prairie northwest of the band of steep river bluffs. Cedar, with the fastest horse, had hurried back to make the riding circles on a ridge where the village scouts would see his signal, and know that buffaloes had been found, some buffaloes, as the narrowness of the circles would show, but enough to bring out some hunters. The small herd was in a good place, so good that with very great luck and a wind shift to the northwest, as could happen toward evening, they might make a little fire drive. The buffalo, weak-sighted, with a mat of wool over the poor eyes, but sharp-nosed, usually moved into the wind to detect any danger ahead. Smoke was such a danger, and a fire could turn the little herd and stampede it over the sheer bluffs into the White Earth valley far below. Even without a wind change the hunters could bring down a few fat cows for extra meat and robes.

Lance and Deer Foot stayed to keep the buffaloes in sight, even try to herd them a little if they started to move fast, get away. A sudden man-smell would send them running, but the young Indians could creep from downwind, perhaps with thick-needled pine branches held before them, moving just enough to disturb the poor eyes of the lead cows a little, make them uneasy and hesitant, turn their grazing sideways. The herd following would turn too, gradually curved back upon itself. Good herd watchers did this very skillfully, sometimes for days, but Lance hoped he would not need to try it and Deer Foot, as always, laughed at the idea. It was not until the work came that he was good.

The two young Indians had hidden their horses in the brush and with their bows slung to the quivers on their backs, they filled the apron flaps of their breechclouts with some drying wild plums still clinging to the naked thickets. Then they settled under a scrubby pine just below the highest crest, where they could watch the buffaloes back on the high prairie and look down over the bluffs to the wide river valley and to the horizon all around. Comfortable in the warming sun, they chewed the dried plum flesh from the pits and spit them at an ant hill nearby, sending the autumn-worried ants running. The youths were excited and hopeful. If they watched the herd well today, they might be asked to go out with the buffalo scouts for the next organized hunt. That was an honor to make one laugh with joy just to think of it, Deer Foot said, but then he sobered.

"Maybe you can go," he said. "You have caught the eagle and killed the three buffaloes. Many big hunters have taken less. You can make the pictures of how the hunt was done. I will have to stay behind to care for my old grandmother."

Young Lance made the sympathetic sound around the

pits in his mouth and offered to look after the grandmother with Cedar the next time. He was examining the horizon under his shielding palm. Suddenly he stopped, spit out the pits and looked again. There was a movement on the bluffs across the valley, something among those pines that always looked like a standing row of warriors along the bluff top, blue-hazed and remote. Perhaps a scout for a Pawnee war party got careless or for some Crows who dared to come clear down into the southern Sioux country.

Deer Foot looked where Lance pointed. Yes, there was something, they agreed, but not an enemy, only a trader's cart, clear against the whitish afternoon sky for a moment before it lurched from among the pines downward on this side, moving like some curious, awkward bug, to vanish in the haze that lay against the rocks and dark trees. Then there was another cart and another, all coming down.

Later the little string of Red River two-wheelers moved out upon the browning fall valley, the carts piled high with trade goods, the drivers sitting on top or walking beside the teams. Behind them came a herd of horses, at least six or seven times the count of the hands, sixty or seventy head, of many colors—acting very uneasy, trying to run, to escape the riders. Perhaps they could smell the water of White Earth River a mile or two ahead, but it seemed to be from up the valley, an alarming sight or sound. Abruptly the lead mares stopped, looking off that way, and then they started to run again, scared by something coming against the east wind. The cart drivers caught it too now, halting their teams, waving their arms toward the west. Lance put his ear to the ground and heard a faint rumbling of many hoofs—the noise of buffaloes running. It was not the small herd they were watching but another, a bigger one far up the valley, and only the east wind had kept the sound from their ears this long.

Then the first buffalo appeared around a far bend, only a

dark speck coming fast, with more crowding behind and more, truly a good herd, massed and dark, the great heads lowered in a stampede that was sweeping down the broadening prairie upon the trader carts. Now the drivers realized their danger and began to yell, their voices in far echoes as they whipped their horses into a run to escape being cut to pieces by the sharp hoofs that no power could turn. The carts bounced and jumped and teetered over the rough prairie, the drivers off and running alongside as they dipped into the brush along the river, crossed in a wild spraying of water and up the near bank, just as the first of the thundering buffalo herd swept past, some with splash of river too, the rest on the dry bottoms beyond in noise and dust and shaking of earth.

The horse herd had scattered like snowbirds on a whirling wind, and turning, ran together again, starting back toward the south bluffs, necks reaching out in the hard run, manes and tails streaming, the lead mares heading them toward their accustomed range. Nothing could stop them now, not until they reached their home region down on the North Platte River toward the mouth of the Laramie.

Ordinarily, Lance and Deer Foot would have laughed at the flight, the riders spurring hopelessly to overtake the horse herd, but now they had other concerns. The far rumble and shake of the earth aroused the small bunch of buffaloes they had been watching until the hunters came. Here and there a cow looked up, then more, and suddenly every animal broke into a run, tail up, galloping eastward into the wind. They swept down a canyon behind the two watchers, dust rising to their horses that faunched in the brush and almost got away before Lance remembered them and ran to grab the rope of his excited buckskin.

The young Sioux were angry over their luck, and uneasy about the start of such a stampede on a drowsy, droning day when most creatures were eagerly feeding for the winter to come. They rode up behind the north bluffs of White Earth River, but cautiously, keeping out of sight, breaking every bend and rise on their bellies. Then from a high point they saw what looked like a substantial little butchering ground, dead buffaloes scattered over the prairie, with men working around the carcasses. Plainly this wasn't a regular meat party, with as many women as men. The youths crept near enough to see the upspringing Crow roach of hair at the foreheads—Crows very far from home and throwing the meat on their pack horses as fast as it was skinned out.

Lance and Deer Foot looked at each other. Crow enemies calmly killing buffaloes here in the heart of the southern Sioux ranges! There were eight or ten men here and surely several scouts out. Even with the hunters who were coming, there would be no more than six or seven Sioux, counting the two bow-armed youths. The Crows would have wasted no powder in their kill but they were sure to have their usual guns along, probably ten or more against seven Sioux bows.

Silently Young Lance led the way down into a brushy draw, hoping no Crow scouts had seen them. Once away, the youths hurried their horses, anxious about this boldness of the enemy. By the time they passed their earlier watching place the canyons were filling with shadow, and still there was no sign of the Sioux hunters. Lance stopped his buckskin.

"It is bad. Perhaps enemies found our friend Cedar," he said. "I must go back; I must keep a wolf's eye on the Crows."

"Alone?" Deer Foot protested. "Somebody must warn the people."

"You go. I shall sneak back."

"It is very dangerous for you alone. They may have seen us, have an ambush made," Deer Foot said, still cautious, as was his nature.

"You will tell where I am, watching, following. You must tell all we have seen, and what must be done. Be careful, and you will be paraded around the village with the news of Crow scalps ready for the taking—a small party among our buffaloes." Then Lance needed to say one more thing, speaking casually while he busied himself with the quiver on his back. "Look after the little Ree if I do not come home."

Deer Foot bowed his head, as though the "Yes" were the most ordinary one. He rode away hiding the concern on his broad face, and disappeared into the brush and timber to make the hidden ride to the village.

When Lance got back to the Crow hunting ground, the cloud in the northwest was rising against the last light of day. He could see no movement except the shadowy slink of wolves and coyotes drawn by the blood and bones left behind, but shying from the man-smell still there or perhaps the men themselves. Lance moved all around the edge of the bluffs and finally down into the darkening valley, crawling through the grass like a snake, wetting his nostrils to catch any smell of hidden smoke. He stopped on a high place to search the darkness for any momentary point of light from a living coal. Now and then he laid his ear to the ground, but there was nothing except the uneven movement of a few feeding animals, perhaps elk. Later he heard the whistle of a lone bull elk, half-hearted, belated in season. Even the sage hens and the rabbits seemed to be gone, nothing rising to flee before the cautious Sioux moccasin.

When the clouded darkness finally shut out everything, Lance settled into a washout deep enough to shield his horse from sight if there should be a flash of fall lightning, the hoofs muffled by the soft sand underfoot. Several times during the night Lance stirred to look around for a sight or a smell of campfire, wishing he had the shirt with the eagle skin for the sharp eyes. Finally he awoke cold and stiff to the gray morning of a storm on the way. He went down to the place of the hunt, with the wolves standing off, waiting for him to go. He found a deep-hoofed trail of loaded pack horses going westward, probably toward Crow country up around the Yellowstone. But that was very far to pack meat. There must be a Crow camp nearer, maybe a large camp preparing an attack. This he must try to find and warn his people, help bring proper Oglala Sioux punishment upon these invaders.

But the small chunk of *wasna* Lance had carried was gone, and before he dared start the long and secret trailing he must get a little meat, particularly with the signs speaking loudly of a new snowstorm on the way. He managed to creep up on a young deer busily feeding, and put an arrow through the heart. He cut much of the meat into thickish slices for fast roasting, packed it on his horse in the hide and took up the Crow trail. He kept hidden as well as he could, grateful for the lowering clouds that ran along the ground and hid all farseeing. Even so, he knew his danger. That night he found a sheltering canyon but afraid to risk even a palmful of fire with its betraying smell of smoke carried on by the east wind, he dug into the warmish sand and curled up to sleep. Toward dawn he was awakened by the soft spatter of wet snow, his horse humped together, head down, rump turned into the wind. Without a robe except the green little deer hide, he could not wait out a storm or the afterward time until the snow gave up the hidden trail. This might not be before spring, and reluctantly Lance started home.

The wind rose with the day, driving the snow from the northwest until it was sharp as trader needles and shut out everything but the sting and cold. Twice it seemed to Lance he must camp, build himself a fire to dry out his worn old deerskin leggings, his thin buckskin shirt, both icy hard. Recalling how deep into the village the lone Ree warrior got before he was seen, Lance felt he must keep moving, warn the headmen as soon as he could. When he finally found the snow-locked circle of lodges he and his horse were ice-caked and barely moving, so stiff and frozen. He was lifted from the horse, stripped of the clothing, wrapped in a robe, wool side in, and taken to the council lodge to tell his urgent story while the frostbite was rubbed from his hands and feet.

Cedar? He was all right, had started back with the hunters. They ran into the buffalo stampeding, and shot meat so long as their arrows lasted.

Feather Woman, his second mother, came with hot mint tea and a lump of brown sugar to warm the shivering young Indian, and whispered to him that the little Ree had sneaked a look in at the lodge flap.

After Lance was done before the council he ate and slept. The next morning he discovered that the trader Frenchy, married to a Brule Sioux woman, had settled his carts and his tipi next to old Sun Shield's lodge. Without the horse herd, he had given out owing sticks to those who wanted horses for the tanned and decorated robes, the sticks to be redeemed later. The carts had brought tobacco, coffee, sugar, hoop iron for arrow and spear points, lead and powder for the few who had guns, some knives, a bolt of fine dark-blue woolen cloth for new leggings and dresses, hawk bells, vermilion for the face, and a little finery for the women. Lance had some furs he had hoped to exchange for a few presents, but everything had been traded away, gone, even the bottle of whisky that was a special gift for the old chief and was doled out around the headmen, a small drink each. It warmed the heart, the trader said, although Good Axe refused his portion. The Axe had been in Bull Bear's village the time a trader brought a keg of whisky there. Before the drunkenness was over, the chief was dead, shot down by a young Oglala warrior.

"It is a memory to shame the face for generations," he reminded the council. "I will not see the blood of our young men heated so again."

But one bottle for all the headmen could do no harm, the trader argued.

By this time the Frenchman's carts were loaded high with robes, ready to start for the trading post on the Laramie River with the first thaw. When the wind dropped and the sun came out a messenger rode in with news that the horse herd had been rounded up at the Platte and headed for the Brule village.

"Why not here?" an angry Sun Shield warrior demanded.

But plainly it would be the Brules first now, for a husband belonged to the woman's people and the trader already had the robes of the Oglalas. Perhaps because there was some resentment about this, the Frenchman started away as soon as possible with his wife, their two children, and Fast Bear, the woman's father, all well mounted, followed by travois and pack horses. The Brule village was two, three days of snow travel away, and soon after they were gone, the scouts signaled Crow sign right in the region—Crows everywhere.

Good Axe, uneasy about his Brule relatives, sent Lance and several warriors to warn them of the skulking enemy. When the party reached the village they found no news of the trader and his family, or of the horse herd, also overdue.

The warriors and Young Lance were taken to the council lodge to tell the story of the Crows. At the first words the headmen sent for a war party to hunt Chief Fast Bear and his daughter and family. Before the men could start, there was a running through the snow-piled village and a shouting that some people were seen coming, some very poor people who had to travel afoot through the deep drifts. It seemed to be a white man followed by an Indian woman and children, with a crippled Indian hobbling along behind on a crutch.

The women hurried out to see and then back to their fires to prepare comfort and relief, murmuring their sympathy as they worked. A dozen strong young men whipped out to help bring the travelers into camp, Lance running too. Even from far off they could hear the woman singing a death song as she waded heavily through the snowbanks, a child on her back, another behind with the hobbling Indian. The white man breaking trail was Frenchy, the trader, his wife singing the thin keening song of one about to lose a loved and respected father—singing for the badly wounded and bleeding Fast Bear.

The rescuers helped them in, women coming to offer their fires, pulling off the snowy, frozen clothing. The Bear, with one legging stiff and red in frozen blood, was carried to the healer's fire, where his wound would be bathed, the bullet drawn out, and the bleeding that had spotted the snow for miles stopped in time to save the man if possible. While the trader and his family were warmed and fed, the council and war chiefs listened to their story. The trader, long on the Plains, had seen no sign of anyone on all the glistening, snow-covered region, but the dawn after the horse herd reached them, the Crows struck, sweeping all the horses away, even those the family had ridden. They did not shoot at the white men but left the Bear wounded on the ground. The Frenchman ordered his herders to follow the Crow trail, but it would take time, for they were afoot.

There was great excitement in the Brule Sioux camp. It was not only very dangerous to have Crows so close around, but humiliating, particularly that they had dared attack a very well-known trader, one who dealt with all the tribes. In addition they had wounded the Bear, related to the white man by marriage, and a prominent Brule war chief. If he died, the war pipe would be carried around all the Plains Sioux for a tribe-wide attack on the enemy, to drive them out, destroy them forever.

While the children, both small, were given frostbite treatment, snow-blind remedies, and heating drinks for their coughing and their burning chests, the war leaders gathered at the council lodge. On a stiff piece of rawhide Young Lance drew a map of the Crow hunting place and the trail with the number of pony tracks on it from there. He also drew a picture of Frenchy's night camp as the trader described it, and of the raid and the tracks. "About twenty or twenty-five men," the war chief guessed when the tracks seemed right to the trader.

In the meantime there were hurried preparations at the warrior lodges. A large party was to drive these invaders out of the country, bring in enough scalps to pay for the insults and the pain, and the wounding of Fast Bear if he did not die—and all the horses they could take. Because such a party must be very well armed, with no time for arrow-making, men came to lay down their extra bows and arrows, war clubs, and spears. Some of those with guns offered them too, although this could not be expected of anyone, with guns so rare. Women brought warm moccasins and bladders of *wasna*, because there must be no hunting, no hunting and no fire that could be detected from any direction. When everything was ready the warriors slipped away in the night, a few at a time, to camp far out so no watching scouts could know a party had gone.

This time no women sang the warriors out of the village, but all knew that their brave-heart songs followed them, songs as strong as their ties to earth and sky. Young Lance went too, and not back behind the men but up ahead because he had seen the Crow trail before the snow and knew the tracks of some of their horses. The war party followed the path of Fast Bear's bloody moccasin that was still plain through the frost-glistening drifts of morning. Grouse in the treetops watched the warriors, moving hidden to anything on the ground, following the tracks as the wolf stalks his prey, sometimes off to one side, sometimes to the other. From the place where the Crows had swept the trader's horses away the trail was easy, with no Indian alive clever enough to cover the passing of so many hoofs in the snow without the luck of wind or new storming. The Sioux hurried on to dark, well past the second night camp of the Crows, and then took up the trail again at dawn. Toward midday the horse droppings became fresher, until even in the snow they were warm inside, steaming in the sharp cold when kicked apart.

By then the Crow scouts, expecting pursuit, had seen the Sioux coming. Outnumbered by the angry warriors riding hard against them, the raiders tried to hurry the laggards of the herd. They whooped the horses along with waving blankets and cutting whips, the flying hoofs throwing up showers of snow. The Sioux kept gaining, and the Crows turned toward the tall gray-white butte standing alone far out in White Earth valley. Because the butte was sheer-faced on three sides, they headed for the scrambling ascent of the fourth, and tried to crowd the horses up the gravelly, loose-rock slide, but each time the lead mare veered off to one direction or the other, and took the herd along.

The whooping Sioux charged across the open flat and divided, streaming up from opposite directions against the Crows, who clung flat against the sides of their horses, shooting over the necks with their many good guns. There was such a tangle of animals and men, so much dust where the wind had swept the snow from the steep bluff side that it was difficult to see and hard to pick off a man without hitting some of the trader's good herd.

Finally three Crow horses were struck and the men had

to jump to others, riding without jaw rope, clinging low. Two of the Brules were hit, one a relative of Young Lance. When his bold warrior cousin went down he no longer saw this as a fine sight to picture, the horses massed close together in their alarm, heads looking one way, nostrils wide, then bolting to this side and that, their manes and tails like blown smoke around them.

Finally one of the trader's tame old mares followed a Crow horseman up the steep slope and over the ice at the top. The rest plunged after her, the Crows whooping behind. A horse slipped with the rider and rolled off the side of the narrow ascent, going over and over, hoofs kicking the air, the Sioux crowding up as the man came plunging after his horse, almost to the feet of Young Lance. Suddenly the youth found the enemy warrior rising up before him, a hand clutching for the knife still at his belt. Lance swung his war club back and brought it down upon the temple of the man. He fell, and the "Yihoo!" of victory rose from the young Sioux throat without effort or volition.

Several times the bolder attackers tried to sneak up the slope, crawling, hoping to get a sight of an enemy to pick off, but each time they were driven back, until the most daring fell with a bullet through the face, dead before the blue smoke spread. The man behind him was wounded too, and so the leader of the party called the warriors back to a safe place.

"We cannot go up against those good guns," he said, angry that their wily relatives, the Crows, had managed to get up the butte. "Too many would die. We must wait. The snow up there is surely very little, the thirsty throats of the men and the horses many."

The others made the *hous* of agreement, sneaking looks up over the edges of their shielding rocks to the men standing boldly erect up at the rim, singing, shouting defiance. Lance saw that there were several boys among them much younger than he, perhaps only twelve or thirteen years old. They jumped rope, shouted in war play, and sang about stealing great herds of horses from the stupid Sioux.

So the men below settled down to a siege, with a guard to watch the only descent. Some rode over to White Earth River with water skins which they flaunted at the cluster of Indians and horses standing dark along the top of the whitish butte, looking a little like the Crow roach of hair springing up from a giant's forehead, arrogant, defiant.

That night Lance lay watching, keeping low so anyone who tried to slip down the only trail would show up against the path of the stars across the sky. He knew it was necessary to keep alert, never take the eye from the one road of escape. He remembered a story that was not included in the heroic tales recounted for visiting chiefs from other villages, other tribes. Paint Maker once showed Lance a little picture of the story, one the old man kept hidden away. In the center was a flat-topped butte* that Lance knew was down in the North Platte valley. A row of Sioux warriors stood before it, stripped to breechclout and moccasins, painted and ready. All were looking up to show that they stood guard. Off to the left, out of their sight, hung a rope, with moccasin tracks leading from it toward the top of the picture and into a gully. The men running into it had the sides of their heads shaved, with only a ridge of hair left standing from forehead to the nape, like the crest of the blue jay. They were Pawnees, getting away.

The story the old man told from the pictures had happened years ago. Some Sioux had surprised a small party of Skidi Pawnees afoot, probably out on a horse raid. With the Sioux whooping close on their moccasins, they had climbed the high rock for safety, their enemies below making the signs for violence and death, and tauntings of cowardice. But the Pawnees wouldn't come down to fight, so the

* Courthouse Rock.

Sioux camped, ready to loaf for a few days until the men on top starved and thirsted, or were caught trying to sneak down. The Pawnees proved very stubborn and must have suffered terribly. Afterward the Sioux heard that in the enforced fasting the leader had a dream vision. "Look for a place where you can get down and save yourself and your men. Look very carefully."

It seemed that the Pawnee crept all around the edge of the butte, feeling his way in the night until he found a point of rock that stuck up a little above the steep wall. With his knife he cut a deep groove around it, letting no betraying dust fall to the ground below. Then he collected the pony lariats that horse raiders always carried around their waists, tied them together and added strips cut from the long flaps of their deerskin breechclouts. When the rope was long enough to reach near the ground he tied it firmly around the groove of the pointed rock and with a hitch around his foot to slow his descent, he started down. Hearing no sound of a watcher below him, he climbed back up and sent his men down, one after another, slowly, it was told later, and silently, bumping against no spot of the sheer rock wall. At dawn the Sioux watchers discovered the patched rope swinging in the rising wind, and the scattering moccasin tracks below it, very light, made by men who crept stealthily away. It was a story told loudly around the trading posts by the Pawnees, and only behind the hand by the Sioux, but nobody ever followed the leader of that Sioux party again.

Now Lance sat looking up at the Crows on a butte and planned a picture drawn with the red earths, and the yellows and blacks of old Paint Maker, but with a different ending. It would be fine to lift the story from the picture skin into words for young ears when he was an old man, recounting the great exploits of the people.

. . .

The sun warmed and the snow began to shrink from the wind-swept ridges, leaving white patches on the slopes and in the gullies. By the third day the Crows on the butte seemed in constant movement, horses running, whips popping, men shouting. One big gray escaped down the slope and was followed by the report of a gun and a thundering crash as he came over the sheer butte face at a bend and landed among the scattering Sioux. The horse lay still in the rising dust, his legs up against the rock wall, a little blood flowing from the small hole where lead had broken the backbone.

"A very good shot," the Brule leader said.

But killing the gray horse did not stop the thirst of the others. Men could survive by cutting the throat of one horse after another and drinking the blood, but for the herd there was no relief. The horses grew more and more desperate, with more and more sound of running hoofs on the rocky top of the butte. The scouts far out in the valley saw the Crows stand in a solid line across the one path down, waving their arms before the crowding horses, evidently cutting the frantic animals across the face with their quirts and ropes to turn them back, send them to gallop around the top, to stop here or there, feet suddenly braced at the very edge of the long, long drop to the valley below. Then they came around again and again, the manes flying about their wild heads, until one young sorrel mare, in the push from behind, leaped into the row of men guarding the descent. She knocked one down and the others fell back from the furious plunge that she led down the steep slope, some of the horses falling and rolling, some sliding on their rumps, others going over forward in the wild surge. At the foot of the butte most of them scrambled up and fanned out on the spreading base into the valley, charging toward the smell of water, toward the river on the heels of the lead mare, red-brown as the fall grasses of the bottoms where the snow had thawed off, her mane and tail a golden sun-touched mist about her.

Most of the Sioux ran for their horses to surround the herd, largely the trader's very good stock. They kept them from drinking too fast, made them feed a little and let them go to the river again. After that the herd was easily held, very hungry and most of them almost tame anyway, saddle-broken.

At the foot of the butte the Sioux danced a little and built up a fine fire, the smoke to rise as a signal of triumph for the scouts far off around the Brule village, and to carry the smell of roasting meat to the starving Crows above. Without food or the blood of the horses it could be only a matter of a day or two until they were forced down by thirst—unless there was a storm, but the snowbirds were bunching again, flying low, and over across the river, elk were moving in their migration to long grass country off southeast.

Somehow those up on the butte seemed undisturbed by the loss of the horse herd—now that it had happened. They even sang a little, the boys playing with their ropes and shouting down to Young Lance, keeping their heads out of sight among the rocks. There was the smell of meat roasting up there too, probably from a butchered horse, and the fine sting of sagebrush burning. The guard on the one path down was doubled, the sentinels watching the fires glow all the night and hearing an occasional little song on the cold air. By dawn there was only silence. Suddenly suspicious, the Sioux circled the butte and found the beginnings of a trail at the foot of a sheer rock face that was taller than the height of fifteen men, and with ropes dangling, reaching most of the way down. The wily Crows had done what the Pawnees did years ago in the North Platte valley, except that these ropes were strips of stout green horsehide from the butchered animals. There were even tracks of a couple of horses that they had evidently kept tied flat on the ground up there, not to be seen from below. Somehow the Crows had lowered them with the ropes too, and slings of rawhide.

Furious, the warriors clambered up the steep slope, Lance with the rest. All they found were the carcasses of the horses and one dog. There was a dead Crow too, an oldish man and still a little warm, but plainly too wounded to climb down the ropes, so he had kept the fires burning and sang his death song. A friend of the Sioux who was killed by the shot in the face that first day took the scalp of the dead Crow. With angry challenges toward the vanished enemy, the rest of the warriors promised revenge and ran for their horses. But it seemed that the Crows had powerful weather medicine. The Sioux, well mounted, followed hard on the Crow moccasins and found where one man had evidently died and was carried along, as was proper. By then the snow had begun to fall again and while the scouts could still find a track now and then on windswept places, they would surely run into an ambush in the thickening storm if they kept going. An ambush with guns against Sioux bows, and no telling how close to all the warriors of the big Crow camp—this was too dangerous.

Besides, they had the herd, as always the property of those who recapture stolen stock, in addition to the Crow mounts taken. They would give the trader and his family their favorite horses, and a very good gentle one to Fast Bear if he was recovering as swiftly as the signals from the village seemed to tell. The rest the party would keep. Lance got three horses as his share, two of mustang stock and still new from the wild herds but tough as rawhide, with tails reaching toward the ground, and handsome as Crow horses must be. The third was a little sorrel mare with a white eye in the snow patch over the side of her face—a pretty and gentle little mare, one that the Ree boy could ride and train as his own.

The return of the party was bad-faced, even with the big lot of horses taken and the two Crows killed, for there was the keening over the body of the dead Sioux. Lance tried to avoid both the mourning and the celebration. He busied himself planning the drawings he would make, all centered on the butte that he was naming for the fight. He would picture the lone high place in the broad valley of White Earth River and show its name by a small figure floating over it—a tiny man with a roach of hair at the forehead—Crow Butte.

Now he, Lance, too would have a picture and a story to hide, like old Paint Maker, with the Crows ahead, but that was only for a little while.

4 / The Hole

THE SON OF GOOD AXE had been called Young Lance ever since the father was selected to carry one of the sacred Oglala lances in battle and in the ceremonials and so was known formally by the customary name of Holy Lance. Now, in the Moon of the Falling Leaves, the son was anxious for a name of his own. He had brought in the little Ree, killed three buffaloes in one hunt, even though they were small ones, and boldly scouted the Crow hunting party alone. For a while he dared hope that one of his fathers or an uncle might walk through the village to sing about these little exploits and give him a new name, a proper grown-up one in place of Young Lance, meaning son of Holy Lance. But it didn't happen, not even after he killed the Crow, which was not really a warrior's exploit, because the man had fallen off the butte and all Lance did was let his arm lift the tomahawk above the temple and bring it down.

What his friends Cedar and Deer Foot admired most were not these deeds but the horses he brought home, and talked of going out to raid a little. Of course no one would let them go, get themselves killed, bring the necessity of avenging them.

"I don't think we should go," Lance said doubtfully. "I am afraid another Ree might come sneaking around."

"Everybody will be watching now. You think you don't need to go because you have all those good horses," Deer Foot said, in his blunt, round-faced way.

"You won't help us get some too!" Cedar taunted.

So three days later Lance found himself looking down upon the cold dawn village of Sun Shield, the lodges coming out in the rising light, the first smoke of the morning fires climbing against the reddening sky. Then he turned to catch up with his two impatient companions motioning him on. They had started away toward the horse herds afoot, as though to help or perhaps to bring in some travois mares for the women to haul wood and water. Instead, they slipped into a washout where the village scouts coming in from the night guard missed them and then ran for a brushy gully and up into the breaks, heading toward the small winter camps of Rees and Mandans and other tribes that might be around the northern part of the Black Hills, tribes long close to the white man. Sometimes they had good American horses, as that larger stock from the whites was called.

When the sun stood halfway up the sky the three young Sioux stopped to rest. Cedar, hunching his thin bones over the little nest of coals of cottonwood twigs, almost smokeless, had big plans. "There will be shining eyes among the maidens when we return with many fine horses."

Deer Foot, the cautious, disbelieving one, said, "Let us catch them first."

Five days later the three young Sioux were scouting the eastern slopes of the Black Hills for signs of smoke against the evening sky and the prospect of good horses in the night herds. The best would be those kept tied to the lodges, and while they might not get any of these, and certainly not the whole herd of their big-talk when they first started, the youths still hoped to pick off at least one good horse each for the ropes wrapped around their waists over the deerskin shirts. The enemy sign they found was plainly of large fall hunting camps, too large and too well guarded these moonlit nights for three young raiders who had never cut a picket rope behind a chief's lodge, had, it was true, never swept away even one foolish colt from an enemy herd on the hills.

The windy fall time made the game too wild for the bow, and as the youths grew leaner, Lance began to wonder about the little Ree, and Dawn, and the rest. His friends were getting tired too, and hungry for a woman's cooking, so they started home, down a wide antelope flat east of the Black Hills. In their hurry the young Sioux were a little careless, concerned by the snow warnings carried by earth and sky and forgetting to be wary where there was no man sign at all, not even old.

Instead of keeping close to the protection of a line of brushy ridges standing blue to the southwest, they cut across the open prairie. Suddenly a party of Rees traveling afoot whooped out of a draw and cut them off. The youths ran for a scattering of creek-bottom willows, but more Rees jumped up ahead of them, turned them to a low roll of barren hills. The Sioux were young and very fast for a while, dodging from washout to buckbrush patch, but an arrow and then more struck beside them. Lance looked over his shoulder and saw that they had run away from most of the enemy, with only three or four close. He slowed a little, to hurry Deer Foot along, and got an arrow into the right knee from behind, doubling the leg under him, so that he went over his head in his momentum down the steep slope. The others stopped to pick him up and held him between them by the arms, dragging him along as he hopped on one leg, the arrow flopping behind the other, the head deep in the bone, the blood hot down his calf. The enemies were gaining now, and sick and weak from the pain and the blood, Lance begged his friends to run, save themselves.

"Look after the little Ree!" he panted. "Run!"

"We must hide you," Cedar managed to say through his tearing breath, and looked around desperately while the Rees were picking up their arrows and sending them flying again. The youths managed to duck over a rise and turned sharply south to a shallow little valley with a strip of weedy ground where a prairie fire had killed the grass long ago. They crawled a while, slowly, touching nothing to shake and betray them to the Rees searching from the ridge, palms shading their eyes. But the enemy must surely find the blood on the grass, and so when the Sioux stumbled upon a large hole in the ground where the butt of a great old cottonwood had burned out in the prairie fire, they left Young Lance. While he crawled in under the dead weeds and grass, dropped into the hole by years of wind, the other two separated and snaked away through a patch of rose-brush and then up a gully that turned sharply northward. They showed themselves a moment, far apart, and although this gave the Rees a dangerous opportunity to cut across on at least one of them like a wolf upon a circling rabbit, it took them far from Lance in the hole. He saw, and for the first time since his cradleboard days he wanted to cry, not from pain or from fear but in thankfulness for these two friends.

Later, Lance dared look out again and saw a Ree running fast over the far rise where Deer Foot had vanished. While he watched the edge of the hole he tried to stop the flowing blood. He found a little movement deep under his thigh, a very little movement like a poor weakening bug kicking deep under a robe, and clamped a thumb upon it. But the pressure only slowed the bright bleeding. He had to stop watching for Ree faces peering in upon him and risk coming out from under the weeds of the hole enough to stop the hot string of blood if he was to live. He sat up against the wall, stretched the leg out, wrapped part of his breechclout string around it above the arrow, and pushed a knot of burnt wood under it, to press upon the faint little pulse as he twisted the string tight. The blood slowed and he tried to clean the wound, working to cut the arrow out of the back of his knee. It broke off and a black wall of pain and weakness fell over him in a kind of dying. When he came alive again in the cold, most of the iron point was still deep in the bone.

With the pain and the weakness whirling about in his head, he felt he had to stretch out. He reached back to dig into the wall behind him with his knife and discovered that his little bow and quiver were still at his shoulder, unbroken. For a moment he forgot the pain and danger in thankfulness. Then he remembered his two friends, perhaps stretched face down in the grass somewhere, arrows in their backs.

Lance was flooded with shame. He had sneaked away from the village, yet all his life he had seen those around him think first of what was best for the people. All the stories told around the lodge coals were about the responsible ones, from those of Holy Buffalo Woman, who had brought the great gifts of the world to the Sioux—the buffalo and all the things of the buffalo. All the stories were like that, down to the kindness that even Arrow Man's widow had showed for the little Ree. Now, when it might happen that no one would ever know what became of them and none to rescue their bones, somehow the bow and quiver had remained on his back through the running, the fall, and the crawling through the weeds.

As the evening darkened, Lance felt the thirst of fever rise in his throat. He dug out some pebbles from the earth behind him and put them into his mouth, but they helped very little. Then he recalled the time of his puberty fasting on the high hill west of Pumpkin Butte. "Lay yourself upon the earth and let all the things of the body blow away, fade away, until you are empty—ready to receive the vision," the holy man wise in these things had said, and his father too. He tried to remember how it had been, naked on that ridge in the burning heat of day, the cold of the spring nights, without fire, food, or water for four days, and the little snows falling like mist to lay on the ground in the moonlight.

The young Sioux tried to stretch himself and his wounded leg out under the weeds and grass in the hole of the burnt cottonwood. He tried to empty himself of the tearing pain and the chills, daring no fire but the fever within him, for surely the Rees would backtrack the trail of his friends as soon as they rested from the killing.

The killing—

Suddenly Lance broke into weak and shaming tears, hating every Ree, even the small one who called him brother. After a while he slept, dreamed, roused, and slept again, and finally it was day. He sat up against the wall, the swollen leg stretched before him, his bow and knife ready, waiting for the dark faces to appear at the rim of the hole. All day he watched, trying to ease the pain until the whitish sky above him grayed and the evening flight of geese passed high overhead, honking quietly. The thigh swelled, hot and hard, but worst of all was the thirst, the mouth dry as an old hide on the prairie. That night a frost fell, and Lance pulled himself up to scrape it like snow from the weeds and grass. It was cooling to the tongue, but there could never be enough to quench the growing thirst.

The next morning a coyote came to stand in the frost-whitened weeds beside the hole, perhaps tolled from the hills by the smell of fallen blood. He dodged sideways once, catching the man scent as Lance moved to draw his bow, but the animal was soon back within arrow reach, sniffing, and when he fell the young Sioux dragged himself out of the hole to the angry creature snapping at this stick that had thrust itself through his flank. With his knife Lance killed the coyote and afterward even risked a little fire in the empty morning. He struck sparks from his flint with the knife back and fed the little blaze carefully, deep under the wall, scattering the bit of smoke with the tail of his breech-clout, impatient, but knowing that none must see a twist of blue rise from a dead weed patch.

He roasted the coyote liver on the coals and offered the first bite on his knife point to the sky, the earth, and the four directions, in thankfulness to the Great Powers in which all things—the rock, the cloud, the tree, the buffalo, and the man—were brothers, all things of the earth and the sky and everything between, a great One together.

The smell of the roasting meat was good only to the starving nose and very difficult for the dry mouth to chew, but the pelt was warm and deep-furred, speaking of a hard winter to come. Lance wrapped it around his shoulders, flesh side out to dry, and slept a little in a restless and feverish dreaming. Afterward he got some roots from the sides of the hole, but there was no water and he was burning with the fire and pain of the wound running through his body. Although there was no sun in the sky now, the snow might be days off, and the nearest sign of water lay beyond the weedy stretch and a bare, buffalo-grazed prairie—too far and too exposed. For now Lance was still sensible enough to know he must wait for the storm.

Late that afternoon he decided on a final risk and managed to toll a curious antelope up close by flapping his leggings over his head, plain for anyone to see. As the animal circled near, he drew his bow, suddenly as hard to bend as the great ones for the buffalo hunts. He let the arrow go. The antelope stood frozen for one breath's length, and then slowly crumpled down. Fearing that he was only wounded, Lance dragged himself over the edge of the hole and crawled through the weeds to slit the delicate throat. He tried to drink the blood for his thirsting, but at first he coughed, choking, his dry and swollen throat refusing to swallow.

Afterward he lay still on the ground, clasping a hand into the weeds to steady himself while he gripped an arm over his quivering, retching stomach, holding it tightly into himself. When he strengthened a little he lifted his head and startled a prairie chicken into a whirring rise upon the air. When she was gone the valley seemed entirely empty, and stumbling to his good leg, he dragged the antelope into his hole as a mountain lion might, but crawled back to cover the blood and the trail so no one passing would see.

By night he had the antelope skinned, the hide hung over the little cave he dug into the side of the hole. There it would shut out the cold and dry for future use. He drank some of the liquid in the watery paunch, sour, but reviving, and stuffed part of the stomach full of grass to dry round as a kettle. Hung from a tripod of sticks, he would boil meat in it, with hot stones when there was water, and there must be water soon if he was to live, even if the wounding could heal. The extra meat he cut into thin slabs to dry and carry along if he had to leave in search of water, or if the hole proved to be too near the trail to the new winter camp that the moving Rees must have made up north. He emptied the antelope bladder, turned it inside out, scrubbed it with sand and blew it up. Dried, it would hold any water he might find.

After the day's work his knee throbbed with a hot pain that ran from his ankle to his hip, and blood and pus seeped from the wound. The next morning he could scarcely move and stayed in the hole. When he caught the sound of hoofs nearing, the steps of two horses, heavy, carrying riders, all he could do was reach for his bow and watch the rim of sky above him. He did not dare hope that these might be Sioux, who would be riding like searchers, not in a straight line going somewhere. He held his breath, the pound of the hoofs and the thump of his heart loud in his ears. Then the riders were past and he risked a look out —two Pawnees, perhaps from a visit to their relatives in the new Ree camp, their trail not over an arrow's flight from his hole.

No more horsemen came for now, and Lance quieted his thirst with a swallow of the sour stomach water of the antelope and tried to sleep, dreaming that there was rain falling. He awoke, lifted the antelope hide. It was snowing, wet spatters falling straight down out of a busy sky.

Although Lance still watched for Sioux scouts out searching, the days passed, the moon darkened, and finally he had to admit that the Ree women must have danced the scalps of his two friends, leaving no one to know where they had been. He grieved for the worry of his parents, for the relatives of his friends too, and for the confusion of the little Ree.

The snow went fast, even though the late fall nights were getting cold. The wounded leg was still swelling, the suppuration gathering deep in the joint, very hot and painful. Finally Lance managed to work his knife into the back of his knee, driving the point into the cartilage over the bone. The searing pain made him clamp his teeth as he twisted and drilled, but carefully not to snap the blade off and be left practically helpless to live. Suddenly the tip went through, pus spurted out, and the pain began to quiet. Afterward Lance tried to clean the infected, stinking wound, cut out the iron arrowhead, but it was firmly imbedded, the thin, sharp point probably bent in the bone.

With the wound opened deep, it might heal some, even around the arrow if he could get to water, more than the little snow he had gathered and covered with weeds against the sun. He must soak the knee, pack the wound with the greenish-brown slime found in old mudholes. Even the bear knew this cooled and heeled a swollen paw.

Toward dusk Lance prepared to crawl out, not certain that there was water at the creek line marked by scattered clumps of brush, or whether he could ever get back from there to the hole. He tied the wolf and antelope skins about him and slung the empty bladder to his waist. Finally he looked all round his little hideout, knowing that this might be the last time he saw the place that had welcomed him, sheltered him so well. More enemies might come along the trail any moment, the way the two Pawnees did half a moon ago, and until he could find a stick for a crutch he could only crawl, not even hobble. Yet somehow his medicine had been good and perhaps it would hold if he did nothing more that was foolish, nothing more like sneaking away from the village. A guilt over the end of his two friends made him want to bury his face in the earth, but there was no time for this now.

Slowly Lance looked all around the prairie and the sky for a sign of alarm. Not even a magpie flew up, or a snowbird, and so the youth started to crawl, moving slowly, cautiously, with pain in the dragging leg. He managed to locate a fall pond in the dry creek bed. There was a little ice left from the morning, and the brownish water was cooling to his throat. Afterward he strained the water through a mat of fuzzy grass tops until he had enough to fill the antelope-skin sack and the bladder. He cut the long back tail from his breechclout, soaked it in the scummy greenish slime at the lower end of the pond, and wrapped it around his knee. The slime stung a little at first but it was soothing too, like puffball dust on a skinned place.

Darkness settled down long before Lance got back to his hole. He rested a while and then hung the antelope stomach on a tripod of sticks, put in water, dried meat, rose hips, and a few arrowhead roots he had managed to find at the water hole. He heated some worn stones from his digging and threw them sizzling into the stomach for the cooking.

With his leg straightened out as well as he could, he leaned back against the wall of the hole and planned. He knew it would be a long, long time before he would see his home village again, his family, the little Ree, Dawn and her pretty friend, Shying Leaf, and the rest. Perhaps never—at least not his two good friends.

Lance had to put this out of his mind, and thought about the animals here. They seemed to be his friends, as in his puberty dreaming, when one after another, small and large, they had come to stand looking at him, seeming to say: "We are your brothers. You will offer your life for a brother many times, and so we offer ourselves." Lance had almost forgotten this, and now he remembered something else: The animals had not gone from his dreaming as animals do, walking or flying away. They had seemed to grow fainter, until they seemed like colored drawings on a skin, like the work of Paint Maker.

From the next skin Lance got he would prepare at least a piece for drawing. It happened to be a weasel, white as the snow of winter except the black tip on the tail, but it was very small.

The moon brightened and began to dim again. By then Lance had killed another coyote, a fox, red as fall leaves, and a second antelope. He dug back deeper under the side of the hole until he had a place big enough to sit up in and stretch out his leg, less painful but stiff as a tree trunk. Small snows chased each other over the prairie and left meltings for the water skin. Then a three-day blizzard swept its whiteness over him, piling the hole full of snow almost before the sun was really gone. All Lance could do was set up a tall bunch of weeds and brush, tied together with grass, at his cave skins and shake it now and then to keep the top uncovered for air. Wood for his small palmful of coals he got by digging out pieces of roots left from the old cottonwood, but he needed very little fire in his earth and fur-warmed nest.

Sometimes he worked much of a short day with his pictures, drawn with charcoal from the old burnt roots of the cottonwood and with blood from rabbits or from his own finger. He drew the pictures and scrubbed them out with a piece of sandstone, and drew again, to capture the look of the coyote and the antelope standing for his arrow, a deepened gratefulness growing in his heart.

He could sleep now, much like a winter badger. The leg drew and burned in its healing sometimes, but it was a cleaner hurt. Even with the pain, he worked to bend the knee as far as the arrowhead, to keep the stiffness that was like stone from spreading in it. When the wind stopped he crawled out upon the snow, so hard it crackled under his weight, the air stinging his nose and chest, the cold so harsh it froze his spit before it fell—his father's way of telling when it was time to stay in the lodge.

Lance never went far after the day he saw the tracks of five horsemen on the trail that the Pawnees rode earlier in the winter. With so much danger he had to be very careful, covering the signs of any move on the snow to look like wind whippings. Rabbits came past on the drifts, and now and then a prairie chicken or grouse stood looking too. By the Moon of the Dark Red Buffalo Calves, February, the leg was healed except for the two holes that seeped a little bloody pus from the arrowhead, the joint still swollen double the size of the other knee, hard and stiff for all his exercising, his rubbing, his attempts to walk. What he needed now was a stout stick with a grass-filled ball of rabbit skin at the top, to fit under his arm.

Then one day the sun was suddenly warm, the snow-banks making busy little noises to themselves as they filled with water that began to run. Here and there the dark earth thrust her back through the drifts to warm herself. Soon the grass would start, and the ponies would strengthen. War parties of Ree and other enemies would ride the prairie trail. Before that day Lance crawled out to the creek, full of water now, water that talked softly to itself as it ran. He found no stick strong enough to bear him but he cut many of the taller, straighter rosebushes, and back in the hole, he fit them together in layers and wrapped them tightly with strips of sinew and then of green hide from the first antelope to return after the storms. The stick dried hard as iron, and with the grass-stuffed ball at the top, he practiced walking.

When the pale moon waited in the east for the sun to set, Lance began to prepare for the long, long journey home, a journey of at least ten sleeps for a well-mounted village, a good hundred of the white man miles, and no telling how many more, with the winter moves the people might have made for wood and game. The cripped youth decided to head toward the forks of the Cheyenne River or the upper White Earth, to seek out old campsites if necessary, with the usual sticks or buffalo skulls to show the direction the village had gone.

He would carry dried meat and the bladder of water and travel mostly in the dusk and on clear nights, nursing the three iron-tipped arrows he had left. He had made a few extra ones during the winter, untipped by the white man's sharpness but with their wood points hardened over the coals. They were good enough even for an antelope if a man's hunger drove him to crawl on his belly like the thin and starving snake that shook no grass as it passed.

Lance bound his knee in a piece of green antelope hide to harden and protect the still festering arrow point. If he could get home, he hoped to find some man with special medicine for strong bones and limber joints. If he could reach a Sioux village, he might still become a warrior, a fitting man for the Dog Soldier society of his second father's youth, a proper son for Good Axe, the honored bearer of the sacred Oglala lances.

But what Lance protected most carefully now was not his arrows or even his knee. It was some neatly folded pieces of painted skin tucked under his breechclout string at the back, out of the way of the bow arm when game was flushed or a sudden attack came. On an antelope skin were pictures telling the winter's story, drawn in charcoal and blood paint worked into the hide with bone and wood sticks. They told of the events beginning with the wounding, pictured in the center, and moved around as the sun moves when a winter-bound man faces southward to the greening time.

Young Lance looked more like a wild man than a Sioux. He was gaunted and shaggy, his hair without the gloss of bear grease or the usual careful neatness in part and braid. He had rubbed his body with snow every few days, but that was a poor cleaning. He had crawled out so often that his well-tanned deerskin leggings had worn out and so he was in the straight, belted, poorly cured robe of the days that the Old Ones told about, before the gift of tanning was brought to the women, and long before the cloth of the whites came.

Lance hobbled out into a shadowed slope, moving very cautiously that first night, suddenly naked of all protection as a turtle that has left the shell behind. But even when the moon climbed higher the prairie seemed empty of all except the skulking coyote that had howled almost every night of the winter. Faithful as a blood brother, he had let Young Lance know he smelled no enemy under the white path of the stars or even under the blazing red sky-fire that climbed and danced up in the north, lighting the way for the coming blizzards.

The young Sioux heard the coyote now, saw him like a swift little shadow on the ridge. He lifted his left hand in the gesture of friendship to his animal brother. Then he started for the ancient lodge-pole trail that ran around the Black Hills, the Race Track as it was called by the tribes. All used the fine, well-watered route, with wood, game, shelter, and much to please the eye. There the young Sioux hoped to find some sign, discover something about the people moving with the spring, about his village and those of the enemies. But he must be careful, for the Race Track was naturally a favorite place for young warriors seeking coups and scalps and horses—a trail of happiness for the well-protected, a test for the careless.

The second evening Lance saw his first buffalo of the winter, a lone old bull on a hillside, probably an angry old one, watchful and desperate. Even if he might be killed by the three metal-tipped arrows Lance could set to his small bow, the mountain of tough hide and meat would only delay his travel. Toward morning Lance heard the first flock of geese, far off in the fading night and high up, but coming, bringing spring on their wings. That meant the ice must be breaking in the rivers.

Around midday Lance looked out of his hiding in a clump of brush to consider a pearling wing of smoke rising on the northern horizon—prairie burning, Indians heating the ground to start the grass for the horses. It was the first sign of a man-being he had seen since the tracks of the riders past his hole, just before the Moon of the Red Calves.

Sometimes it had seemed that he was the only human being in a white and frozen world.

Lance moved slowly and cautiously even in the dusk, careful that his one foot and the strong ash crutch he now used left no imprint on soft earth if he could help it, no tracks to cry the news of an easy scalp. Perhaps he should have gone to the French trader's place off east of his hole, closer but certain to have Rees around, even Mandans and Poncas.

He had traveled five nights when he caught a glimpse of light, no more than a firefly's, and gone as quickly. But this was red, light from a fire coal. He stopped, easing himself into the grass, afraid he might already have been seen by someone back from the camp, curiously afraid even if it were Sioux. He crawled carefully toward a ridge of earth that stood against the horizon and settled into the first little draw to wait. He couldn't see the bit of fire again, but he would not let himself believe, easily, that he imagined it. "Trust your eyes and ears—they are your friends," the old ones repeated to every child, long before the small heart could understand the words.

Afraid to move and too uneasy and too cold to sleep, Young Lance found the night a long, long one. As the east lightened he made a cap of grass for himself, large enough to fit down over his face too, with slits for the eyes and ears. Slowly he lifted his shielded head into the wall of similar grass at the edge of the draw and looked for movement where it seemed the fire had been. He watched the gray little valley come out of dawn. Half a dozen silver-breasted grouse chattered amiably in the top of the old cottonwoods at a little creek that looked dry. Something disturbed the birds, started an angry cackling, their small heads turned to look down the creek where a coyote sneaked up through the weeds on his belly. Suddenly two grouse burst from a clump of rosebrush barely beyond his nose, their short wings whirring hard as they flew up, then quieted in their soaring eastward into the first hard rays of the sun. The grouse in the cottonwoods lifted and followed. The coyote looked after them, his nose in the air, and then he trotted sullenly to a rise, perhaps to get out of the way of a gray wolf traveling the ridge on the far side of the creek.

With these signs that there was no man-smell on the wind blowing toward him, Lance dared creep out, and stooping low, hobbled to where the fire had seemed. He found a little earth-covered spot the size of two hands below a brushy bank. He pushed the dirt and ashes aside and flattened his palm on the burned earth. It was cold, the few moccasin tracks around covered too, so only those who knew they were there could find them at all.

Feeling thankful to the little fire gleam that had showed itself to him last night, he crawled into a draw to sleep, but one last look around the horizon made his heart jump like a rabbit's in a man's palm. An Indian on a gray horse was riding down a little canyon from the west, with more heads behind him, the men coming into sight plainly a war party. Ten men, with at least four, five scouts out. As the string of riders neared, Lance saw that two had the sides of their heads shaved, with the crested ridge of hair worn by the proud Pawnee warriors, and knew that if he was detected, he was a dead Sioux.

Holding his breath, Lance turned his staring from the men so he would not draw their eyes. Instead, he watched the spot of the little fire, where he had foolishly left his fresh moccasin tracks. When he dared look at the party, they were crossing the little creek well past the fire. The leader carried a gun across the withers of his horse, and the one behind him did too. All were painted; most of them had fine long bows, filled quivers, and shield cases. Two bore lances. They came up the slope, closer and closer, heading for the ridge just above Lance, the one direction from which his hiding was no hiding at all. If even one horse caught his scent and lifted an ear—

All the youth could do now was to flatten himself into the weeds of the draw, face down, so no blink of an eyelid might catch the attention of man or horse. He made himself empty as Jumping Moose advised his scouts. "Be empty and without skin, so no one can capture the thought of your body, of you."

Young Lance heard the steady fall of hoofs coming almost straight for him, and the easy talk of men. Then there was a sharp word to a horse, and the stopping of movement, with surely every man looking. Now it was hard to hold himself as nothing, as empty and nothing. Next, one of the men made a sound that seemed a direction, a word to go with a pointing, and then another word, one from the French traders that all the Plains people knew: "*Loup!*" Wolf! They had seen the wolf, and the horses from the end of the line—the younger men—sprang into a run, a wolf chase.

But some of the hoofs did not move and Lance waited, making his mind blank of that other exclamation that might come, the one that told of his detection. Or there might be only a stealthy approach, a man falling upon him with a knife, or an arrow finding him. A spot in his back began to ache, one where a bullet or an arrow or a spear would strike, until it seemed to Lance that he must move, must shield his vulnerability where man has neither fur nor shell.

There was a word, a growled one. The horses started, but not toward him; the slow hoof fall was drawing away down the other side of the ridge. After a long, long time Young Lance dared to turn his head a little, to clear an eye of the sting of earth in it. There seemed no one around, no one around anywhere.

When he was certain that the last Pawnee was gone, he lifted his open, defenseless palm to the sky, turned it to the earth and around in all directions in gratitude to the Powers in which all things of earth and sky are brothers.

Then he crept down to the little fire to hide his foolish moccasin tracks and on into a clump of rosebushes, which carry a little scent of their own, help hide a man's smell. He covered himself with the dead weeds and brush so none could detect him unless a foot struck his flesh and bone.

He traveled as fast as possible that night, first into the wind like the buffalo and then with it as the blowing shifted to the east, driving into a storm. At dawn he sought a good hiding place, one where he could watch the horizon for signs of morning fires in a village. He saw a wide frost haze low on the southern horizon, far off—a great buffalo herd, the steam of their breath and bodies a cloud on the freezing air of morning. It was a happy sight, a reassurance that the good life of the buffalo Sioux was not just a fevered dream of the Ree arrow under his knee. Still, buffaloes drew enemies as well as friends.

He saw no threads of smoke or any smudge of it. Heavy-hearted, Lance settled to his hiding. There was no sign of his people, and a storm was surely very close, the snowbirds flying up like fall leaves on the wind, and then settling back in their watchful circles, feeding busily. By evening wet snow slapped his face as he started out again. Caution told him to find shelter, with a little wood, to wait out the storm, but a curious impatience a little like the need to migrate that drove duck and goose, elk and buffalo, in the spring, pushed him on. The storm thickened with the day and travel sideways to the northwestern wind became more difficult, the leg and its crutch dragging in the deepening snow. The danger of being seen, however, became less when the hand before the face was lost in the driving whiteness.

Lance was about exhausted and ready to search out a hole somewhere in the broken country around him, one he could clear of snow enough to shield a handful of fire. Then his frozen nose caught a whiff of smoke. He stopped, crouching down to catch it near the earth, and found nothing. Afraid to move now, he stood, and the smoke came again, this time with the fragrance of sage and sweetgrass in it—village smoke, or at least of a camp large enough to feel secure, one with women and woman food and comfort.

But Lance realized that the village could be Crow or Pawnee or even the wandering Rees. He tried to think of some way to make certain, and heard the far hoot of an owl, a scout's hoot, and the swift, muffled thud of hoofs in the snow. He drew back shivering from more than the storm and cold. A rider passed him like a pale shadow in the blizzard wind, and then a second. There was something familiar about the second horse, even snow-caked and hunched together. He knew that horse. It was his own buckskin.

Without thinking, he shouted, and then clapped his hand over his mouth. The horse could have been stolen. But no caution would stop his weary foot, his snow-impeded crutch, now. Suddenly no longer tired and stiff as wood from the cold he hobbled forward, stumbled, and was grabbed from behind. Without willing it, he struck out with his knife, but his free hand was trapped, twisted back, his face turned up in the snow.

"It is the Lost One!" the Sioux scouts exclaimed. "It is the Young Lance!"

So he was carried to the soldier lodge, and the crier sent running among the storm-hidden lodges shouting, "One who was lost and called dead has returned living! The one called Young Lance is back!"

5 / In the River Country

THE MEDICINE MAN shook the snow from his beaded holy mantle and stooped under the lodge flaps with his frostbite cures. Outside, men and women with their robes over their heads against the storm gathered for news. Moccasin and the two mothers hurried over, asking how Young Lance was, and where he had been this long time, Cloud Woman, the blood mother, with reserve, the second mother with more freedom, more permissible warmth.

"Our brother, Good Axe, is away far south of the Platte with the Brules, making plans for the Sioux nation, and for an attack on the Rees when the ponies strengthened in new grass," Moccasin said. "In his place we welcome our son's return. It is good that we have no dead relative to avenge." The man spoke with formality, covering the concern they felt for the crippled and frozen one.

Yes, oh, yes, Lance was told, Deer Foot and Cedar had returned safely, confessing that they sneaked away and lost their friend to the Rees. They took their punishing blows from the village police and listened to a harangue on the dangers they had brought upon themselves, and the mourning upon the relatives and friends of Young Lance. Because the Rees were moving in a big camp through the country, the youths had been commanded to wait with their return to the hole where Lance was surely dead. After the mourning time, when spring came, they could guide a party with the proper red-painted skin sack to gather up the bones of their friend for the tree or the scaffold. Then was the time for the avenging.

And now Lance had returned, crippled, gaunt as a starving coyote, and with feet frozen, particularly the unused one. But he was alive, and people were already coming to bring the owing sticks for the return of the horses the father had given away for his son lost. He had cried out: "My heart is on the ground! My horses are for those who will take them!"

All had been accepted except the father's hunting mare and those that belonged to the women of the lodge. Now all these were to be returned, but the mother gave away most of the owing sticks in joy to the needy.

Half a moon later Lance could hobble on his good leg. His feet were still swollen and dark as the bluish-purple berries that ripen on the steep bluffs of summer. His toes, the outsides of his feet, and the heels bulged with yellow pus spots that pained and burned until opened. These holes would heal very slowly, Lance knew, and the itching of the frosted flesh made him scratch and dance every time his feet warmed. But Feather Woman, the second mother, knew how to make the healing salves and lotions and soon there was only the long slow festering. By this time Lance was getting acquainted with the little Ree again. The boy had grown, spoke Sioux now, and had truly become a brother to Cub and the teasing twin sisters, even while Lance was considered dead from a Ree arrow.

"They became angry with me when you were first lost,"

he said once, the only indication that he realized his danger if Lance had been a prominent warrior or an honored man in the village. Then one little Ree might have had to die to make some foolish heart good again.

The winter had been a watchful one, with raids on the horse herds by Crows, Pawnees, and Rees. Eight good men had died, men Lance had known all his life. But they upheld the Sioux tradition. There were forty more Crow horses among the herds up on the hills, and some big ones from the Pawnees. Eighteen coups were counted by the young warriors, seven daring ones on living men, the rest on those killed. One of these, a Crow, was shot by Deer Foot while guarding the horses. He saw the man creep up on the snow under a white cloth and put an arrow through him.

The heavy spring snows went fast in the climbing sun. Soon there would be grass and the horses strong enough for raids and war. It was time to move from the last winter camp. The wood was gone, even the young cottonwood branches brought in for the green bark that the horses gnawed while the grass was drifted under. Only the American horses, those good ones from white man herds, had to have grass cleared for them or cut and dragged home over the snow. Not only the wood and grass was used up around the village; the ground had been very worn and was certain to stink in the first really warm day.

With the snow almost gone, there were ceremonials and the big dances for the young people that drew visitors from other Sioux villages riding in, and a big party of Cheyennes. Young Lance couldn't join the circles, not with his swollen feet and his knee still stiff although the arrow had been cut out, the bent and rusting point of hoop iron gone.

There was one ceremonial and feast he could attend, the one at the lodge of Dawn, the girl who had suddenly grown shy and womanly. Last fall she was almost as bold as a boy. Once she had leaped upon a big bay and whipped it at a high run through a prairie-dog town, sticking on as the horse dodged this way and that to avoid stepping into the open burrows and perhaps breaking a leg and the girl's neck.

But now she had gone through the puberty ceremonial, and so the crier ran around the village circle to invite all the family friends to a feast. The girl's father had been to Frenchy, the trader on the Laramie River, with four pack horses of prime winter furs, and brought back finery for his daughter who had become a woman. There was also much tobacco, coffee, the brown sweet lumps that were called sugar, and flour for the fried bread. A woman among them here had been the wife of a trader on the Running Water and knew how to make the bread, which was very good with coffee and sweet lumps in the cup.

Lance felt bad-faced that he could take no fitting present to the pretty girl who had beckoned him into the dancing last fall and then sent her glances past him to the tall, lean-faced Cedar, who had been so embarrassed that he slipped away in the darkness. But Lance noticed that this too had passed.

Now Dawn sat in the back of her new ceremonial lodge, in fine doeskin, the blue-beaded yoke deep as her heart, her face pretty with vermilion, the braids hanging neat and shining under the long shell-core bands, the part in the hair ochered as it would be by her husband someday, as every good husband did.

Lance had to wait his turn to get close enough for a word of good wishes. Dawn's mother, her sisters, and friends sat with her, and the wisest man of the village was making the customary harangue, praising her beauty, her talents, her warm and dutiful heart as a child, and counting out the responsibilities and duties of her womanhood to her family, her village, her tribe. "If the virtue of the women is lost, the buffalo will fail," he said. "Let your moccasin tracks never fall anywhere except on the good road."

Before Dawn lay a pile of gifts, a robe of otter skins to shed the storms and to move with the grace of her walk, blue-woolen cloth for the dress that was to be decorated by the elk teeth of her husband's gifts someday. There were strings of beads the color of every known bird and flower, and rings, bracelets, ribbons, and more long shell-ornament bands to hang from the braids. Behind Dawn, fastened to the lodge wall, was her own beadwork, including moccasins for her future husband and the handsome saddle trappings for the horse she would now ride among the young women in the parades and village moves.

All Lance had to add to this was the white weasel skin, barely larger than his hand, with a picture painted on the underside, deliberately done, with lines fine as maiden's hair, in black, reds and yellows, and a white that was like snow. It was a picture of one of his dreams of the Holy Buffalo Woman who had led the Sioux to the country of the great herds. In his turn he laid it diffidently upon the pile before the girl and backed out to limp to where the other youths gathered for the feasting. Lance ate very little, for there were young warriors with many coups standing around, and later, when darkness came, there were even more for the singing and dancing around the big fires. Dawn seemed everywhere in her handsome blue-yoked dress, lifting her soft eyes, her smile to this and that warrior. Lance saw, and slipped away to one of the wickiups behind the village, and was as much alone as in the hole where an old cottonwood stump had burned out.

The next day Good Axe returned from his conference with the Brules below the Platte. His unbelieving surprise and joy at finding Lance alive stopped him halfway off his horse, standing there as on air for the time of a heartbeat. Then he let himself down, handed the rope to his wife and walked to the youth, looking carefully into his face.

"You are alive again," he said, very quietly. "It is a second living!"

The next afternoon the crier came shouting through the village. "Listen, people, listen to this!" Behind him walked Good Axe in the dignity of his beaded ceremonial robe, the one feather of his honored place as bearer of a sacred Oglala lance standing straight at the back of his head. He was singing a song over and over:

"Our son known as Young Lance has returned,
Our son, wounded and alone in a freezing hole,
Has made himself live when we accepted him dead.

"I give him the name of Lone Lance,
A strong name, for one who can stand alone."

Lodge flaps were pushed open, old people looked out, and some began to gather behind the moccasins of the singing man until it seemed that all the village was coming toward the young Sioux who had been sitting in the sun working his knee back and forth.

He stopped when he saw the crier come, and his father and all the people, and his face grew set and distant, so the crying inside did not show through.

When the geese were flying thick and would surely be dark on the waters of the Platte, Sun Shield's village started in that direction. The hunters had rolled up their furs, the women their robes, all ready for the traders, everybody planning what these might bring in hoop iron for spear and arrow points, in powder and lead for the few guns, even perhaps bring another gun or two. There would also be good horses, blue and red cloth for leggings and dresses, beads, paints, hawk bells, knives and kettles, and all the good white man foods.

One afternoon the pipe bearers leading the moving people stopped on a little creek flowing down into the North Platte. The scouts had signaled that a village was camped up the river on the other side, and that the people were those who hung around the traders at the Laramie. These were called Loaf About the Forts by those who preferred the old free hunting life instead of the presents from traders and the soldiers riding through, presents for giving the white men the prettiest maidens as wives. Often the presents included much whisky, as had happened out along the Missouri River long ago and convinced many Sioux chiefs that they must take their people far away, out upon the plains.

There were several relatives of Sun Shield's village among the Loafers, and the first afternoon Star Woman and a friend wanted to ride over to see their new grandchildren. The scouts, however, reported that Le Noir, a trader that the Indians called The Black, was in the Loafer camp with a load of whisky. He had already obtained bales of furs and robes, enough to pile his wagons, and there were more whisky kegs standing in his tent beside the lodge of old Two Palms, the former chief. It was a pleasant afternoon, and Moccasin asked Lance to go with the two women who wanted to visit over there. They had only old men in their families. "You are young for this task," the youth's second father said, "but you will not be drawn into ancient disputes with the drunken ones and you can see what must be done without being told."

Honored, Lance hurried to get ready, eager to see the new things these Loafers would have from the traders.

Besides, there would certainly be a cup of coffee filled half full with the sweet lumps or perhaps a few of the big dried grapes called raisins, or some other visitor's treat.

As he limped in for his robe, Feather Woman stopped to warn him. "Be careful, son. There is much whisky there, we hear, and if fighting starts, people will be killed. You must try to get the women out—"

The trail led through sandy hills with the first greening of spring running along the southern slopes. Ducks swam the water-filled buffalo wallows. A golden tinge misted the willows along the creek where the swelling buds would burst into furry mole paws, and a brightening lay on the young cottonwoods where tassels of bloom would flutter in the wind. The river was flooded but Lance's buckskin took it easily, swimming strong, heading upstream to hold the line of the ford. The women behind drew up their legs, laughing a little, secure on their good horses too.

Lone Indians stood on the rises east of the village, their blankets about them, perhaps singing songs of praise and joy or of sorrow. Out in the valley a lot of stripped young men were running and shouting in a fast stick-and-hoop game, while up among the horse herds youths of Lance's age were whipping ponies back and forth, preparing for the longer races of the summer, when the horses were strong and the betting posts stood rich in wagers. Near the village of winter-smoked lodges more youths were gathered, some running in groups, some splashing in the cold river flood. Smaller boys swarmed in excitement, throwing arrows at buffalo chips or clumps of weeds ahead of them, the winner taking all. Others raced, their long hair and breechclouts flying, or stalked birds and rabbits, their bows arched ready if any should appear.

But in the village it was different. There were packs of dogs, as was common among Indians clinging around traders, where barking betrayed no one to an enemy. Today the dogs just slunk around or stood at the lodges, silent, looking. No young girls walked laughing through the camp circle or over the pleasant prairie. Few women were out; none cooking, none working robes and beading, nor even sitting around the gambling robes spread on the ground, the women shaking the plum-pit baskets, wagering anything from the simplest trinket to horses, and sometimes even a husband. Many of the men, middle-aged and old, sat beside their lodges, perhaps singing to themselves or curiously silent and brooding. A few smoked and talked, perhaps talked a little more than usual from The Black's whisky, but that was all.

Lance was uneasy as they rode into the camp, the women behind him making concerned noises, particularly when they passed two young men sprawled in sleep at a warrior lodge, their hair and faces dirty, perhaps from repeated falling down.

"Let us go back," one of the women whispered.

But the visitors had already been seen by a relative, running out to take the horses. Lance shook his head, smiling a little, but determined not to be separated from his buckskin mare yet. She was good in a fight he knew from the time at Crow Butte. She had stayed quietly beside him when other horses tried to get away.

Before Lance found any of his acquaintances, the stink of people breathing whisky in the village made him decide to go up to the horse herds, but a woman came running out, calling: "It is the son of Good Axe! Welcome, my son!"

She motioned him to a seat at the lodge door and brought out a wooden bowl of raisins. He filled his mouth in the sign of appreciation and appetite, savored the sweetness and cracked the seeds. While the woman asked about his parents she tried to keep him from noticing the people at the next lodge. A young man stood beside the door there with his robe over his head, as when the heart is bad. An old woman who seemed to be his mother sat on a tree stump beside him, talking directly to him as no mother should to her blood son after his early boyhood. She swayed on the seat, plainly drunk, her whining voice rising and falling in repeated complaint.

Lance ate raisins and visited with the friend of his family, happy that this woman was sober and good. He answered her gentle questions about the health of the twin sisters and about the captured little Ree who made a sort of twin for his young brother too. Her concern about the crippled knee was interrupted by a scream from the old woman at the next lodge. She was pointing to a wrinkled, gray-haired man riding a gaunt and shaggy pony through the camp circle. "There goes a bad man!" she cried to her son. "Thirty winters ago he made me weep and brought sorrow to your brothers and sisters too, for he killed your father!"

The young man threw the robe from his head, jerked the pistol from his belt and fired one shot into the old man's back. The man stiffened and tumbled from his pony. At the report, the spreading blue smoke, cries of anger and alarm cut through the camp. Immediately everyone grabbed for weapons, women too, snatching up spears, bows, or drawing their long butcher knives. At the roar of anger the young man took one lurching step and was suddenly very sober. Realizing his danger, he ran for the bluffs behind the camp, arrows and a few bullets striking around him as he zigzagged and dodged this way and that. Lance, forgetting the women he brought, ran with the pursuers. He saw the man reach the breaks just ahead of the running crowd, the shots and the arrows so close that he was struck several times as he got into the rugged bluffs. He scrambled through a gully and over a bare ridge until he reached a narrow ledge of rock where no horse could follow, the ledge high enough to overlook the village, the top covered with boulders and stunted pines. Perhaps the fleeing man knew he was badly wounded. He didn't hide, but stood up for a while, a plain target. He even returned some of the arrows that hailed around him, holding back the angriest of the Indians by pointing his pistol, loaded or empty, none could tell.

The man's brother and some others sneaked around the bluff and worked their way up behind him, advancing cautiously from tree to tree until the man on the ledge saw them. "Not you, my brother!" he shouted. "Do not come to bathe in my blood too!"

But the men kept advancing, perhaps anxious to get the killer before more died and brought avenging. Suddenly the man on the ledge sat down, and something dark began to drip over the narrow stone, one dark drop, another, sandy but plainly blood as it fell close to those hidden below him. Lance could hear the brother calling from the pines for surrender, warning him he would surely be killed out there. But no reply came, only the silence of waiting. Then the wounded man pushed himself to the edge of the high cliff and looked down upon the crowd below. With his face bloody, he sat there almost motionless until an arrow struck his shirt at the heart. He held himself for another breath and then he sagged slowly forward, toppled over the ledge and fell spread out, the Indians staggering back out of his path.

The dead man's uncle stepped forward, joined by the brother leaping down the bluff side. With four, five others, they picked up the body and carried it back into the village, many who had just howled for the man's blood now falling into the silent row behind him. Lance went too with some of the village young men, including some from the hoop game and the racing, all stopped by the first shot.

In the village Lance heard a wild keening such as he had never known before, with a whisky heightening of the grief for the two men suddenly dead. It helped stir a new anger in the gathering Indians. Lance felt it grow around him and hurried for his horse, to ride to the lodge where the women visited, but he was cut off by the surging crowd now roaring against the trader who brought the whisky.

Apparently The Black had known that the old chief was not powerful enough to offer protection after two killings from any trader's firewater—not against the march of angry men led by those burning with the same whisky. The old chief's women saw the crowd come. They dropped their lodge, piled it on travois poles and dragged it away to the protection of the war chief, and stood there beside it, confused and helpless, watching the trader's tent go down in fire. Spears and axes were struck into the whisky kegs, the fire following the spilling liquor, turning its flow into streams of blue flame. The trader wagons were pushed into the fire too, but only after some of the sober men threw the bales of furs and robes off, to be returned to the Indians. In the meantime others were kicking their way through the lodges searching for the whisky peddler. With war clubs raised they demanded that the old chief tell where the man was hidden. Finally one of the frightened old women admitted she had seen The Black slip away into the brush of the river, carrying his gun. Some started after him, but most of the bow-armed Indians hesitated, milling around angry and sullen, quieting a little.

One of the young men who had been sleeping off his whisky beside the warrior lodge roused up, saw himself surrounded by dark faces, by armed and angry men. He crawled into the lodge and fired one shot out into the people. His aim wavered, but he pointed the barrel into the thickest crowd and brought down a woman. At the new shot and the hit and crying, knives flashed out, war clubs were raised and arrows set to the bow. The village split into factions, fighting hand to hand, bloody ones falling, lodges flaring up in fire.

The horses of the two women with Lance had broken

loose long ago, and so he cut the rope of the only horse he saw still tied in the village, hurried it to the lodge where the women cowered in the dark interior. He got them both on the one horse and whooped it into a run ahead of him, the women clinging on as well as they could. Some of the mounted warriors, seeing them leave and not knowing who they were, started after them, shooting. Lance flattened himself to the back of his buckskin, whipping the horse of the women along faster and faster, with men still charging after them. The horse guard on the way in tried to cut them off, not understanding what was happening. Once Lance lifted up to motion everybody back, and got a lead ball through the skin of his upper arm. The drunken leaders kept right on coming until they fell off or played out. The horse guard, perhaps seeing that two of the fleeing ones were women, stopped and looked off toward their village where more fires blazed up and more shots echoed.

Lance got the women away into a shadowed canyon and kept along it until darkness, and then rested. It was late when they reached camp. Lance had signaled their distress to the scouts, and the headmen were ready at the council lodge to hear the story the women told, murmuring in anger, and recollecting the time the drunken twenty-year-old Red Cloud, a visiting warrior in Bull Bear's village, killed the chief. A trader had sent a keg of whisky as a gift to the Sioux, to draw them close—whisky enough to bring death to the chief and six or seven others, with many more wounded, and a split in the Oglala Sioux that might not heal for many lifetimes.

The councilors raised their voices against The Black and his trading, particularly Sun Shield, his dark, high-nosed old face lean in anger. Whisky made fools of men. No wagon of the kegs would ever be permitted in his village so long as he wore the fringed shirt of responsibility.

In the wickiup later Lance tried to find a comfortable

position for his arm cut by the ball. He thought about the day and of the killing of Bull Bear, and what happened afterward. It seemed that because it happened through whisky, there hadn't been the proper banishment for the killing that even repeated little troublemakings could bring. Lance recalled the orders always given to the warrior society selected at the time of the new moon to police the village until the next moon came. He liked to hear Sun Shield repeat the words in his deep, quiet voice. "Where every lodge is open there can be no thieves; where no man's word is cut in stone, no liars. Our people live very close together, and there can be no troublemakers in the village and no violence upon body or life. For the first small wrongs, there is to be the warning, for the second, a bow struck across the shoulders, publicly, for all to see. If the troublemaker persists, he will be driven out for as many moons or winters as seems wise to the council. Violence against the body and against life must bring banishment from the entire Sioux village, even as long as the holy number of four winters."

"The lance of power and justice is given into your hands for this moon's time. Treat it with honor."

"Treat it with honor—" Lance wondered where the police were in the Loafer village today. Perhaps all that lawlessness would be blamed on the whisky too, as it was when Chief Bull Bear died. Lance had seen two drunken men come into Sun Shield's camp once, sodden and quarrelsome, but they had been taken away into the hills and not brought back until the next day, sick and ashamed.

Sleep did not shut out what Lance had seen in the Loafer village. The next morning he begged a deer hide from Feather Woman and drew the pictures of the shootings, the milling crowds, the burning, the loose and foolish faces, the silly old woman blaming an old man for a thirty-year-old crime against a son not over twenty.

In a few days three of the Loafer council came in formal array with their escort of young warriors—the relatives of the women Lance had taken there and the friend of Good Axe who had welcomed the youth with the raisins. The Loafers brought the two horses the women had lost and a pack load of food and finery as an apology gift. For the wounding of Lance, slight as it was, they brought a good young stallion, one they got by trade from the white emigrants when he was still a foot-worn little colt. This big gray would head the fine herd such a steady and stalwart young man should have.

"A crippled young man, one who cannot become a glorious warrior," Lance told himself, but he made his quiet words of gratitude.

The spring days around the trading post at the Laramie River were gay ones for the young people. There were several other Sioux and some Cheyenne and Arapaho villages camped on the worn earth, so worn that most of the horse herds were out two or three sleeps to the north and northwest, with strong warrior guard.

There were big bull trains coming up the Platte with the usual goods for the spring Indian trade, including the dark-blue blankets that the chiefs were taking up in place of the heavier buffalo robes. There were traps too, for the few beaver left, and for the otter, mink, and wolf, but these were usually loaned to the Indians, to assure the trader the pelts they caught.

After the closed-in winter, the Indians liked to wander through the trader houses in the daytime, wishing, planning. Evenings, even the older ones went to the dances in one camp or another or perhaps stopped to look in where their friend Frenchy played the fiddle and one of his helpers the pull box—the accordion—for the white man's way of dancing, the cloth skirts of the pretty breed girls flying out as they whirled past in the arms of the white men. This year Lance kept away from both kinds of dancing and took his turn with the nearby horse herd the first night that Sun Shield camped near the traders, when no one else wanted to go. The next day he wandered around the houses a little, looking, and was ready to leave when Star Woman, whom he had taken to the Loafer village, called to him.

"For the young man who helped get us away from the whisky fighting," she said, holding out a slender black box, the lid raised. Inside was a row of color sticks, two each of yellow, red, blue, and black. "For the drawings, the pictures."

Lance stood holding the box, still open, just as he had accepted it from the woman. "One is thankful," he said gravely, and backed away. He walked slowly at first, watching his limp, then faster and faster, until he was taking great leaps on his good leg. He had not known that there were such color sticks in all the world, fine bright colors, each longer than a finger.

He saw the little Ree playing with Cub and other children at the river and called to him. Lance had been warned to keep the boy hidden around the trading post, where every tribe might come, and many traders on their way to the northern posts. In the shade of a leafing cottonwood Lance tried the color sticks, the little Ree making odd designs new to Lance, pictures that he said were corn—long ovals like corn ears, but marked off by cross lines, the squares filled in with red and blue and yellow. Lance gave the boy one of the two red sticks to keep, to show his right to the colors too. Then he turned Cub over to the other five- and six-year-olds and kept the little Ree with him as much as he could until the night of the big dances for the Loafers, invited with their best songs, handsomest finery, and most expert dances, but without whisky, as Sun Shield's messengers had made clear. The Loafers came at dusk, singing, painted, with whitened robes or blue blankets folded across their horses, their young women painted and handsome. Two of the party pounded drums while the rest sang the riding songs and whooped as they charged into the village. The young warriors stepped forward to greet the guests, the maidens out too, looking shyly from their blankets while the young women made the welcoming trills and the older ones came to take the horses.

Lance limped around to the drumming, the singing, and the dance fires to look after his twin sisters, still young and at the fringes of the gaiety but moving inward. He couldn't see Dawn at all for the admirers around her and her friends, so he slipped away to his horse and rode to the nearby night herd, announcing himself to the leader: "If it pleases you, tell Deer Foot someone has come to take his place. Tell him to go to the dancing."

Lance was sent to the far side of the herd, with his bow and knife handy. There he could hear only the loudest cries of the gay evening, barely catch the drumming with his ear to the ground. He had come to hide his crippling in darkness, to open his heart to an understanding of what must be done. There was still a small wound in the back of his knee, and perhaps it was this that prevented the supple bending every good Sioux warrior must have. He spread his robe near the crest of a ridge that overlooked the western slope and settled down on it, squatting as low as he could with the stiff knee. Then he forced himself lower, up and down again, slowly, silently, giving no sign in the darkness of the pain that shot to his toes and up his leg, even to the shoulder. He kept this movement in time to the heart sound, up and down, until the leg was numb. Then he stretched on his back, drew the knee up as far as he could, and pulled it farther with his strong arms, let it go and pulled again, until there was heat and swelling. He walked a while, keeping below the horizon line of the ridge, stepping firmly on the leg for all the pain and cramping. Slowly, silently, he moved back and forth, straining his eyes up to where the horses were feeding and over the dark plain to the west.

It was then that he caught the first movement on the slope below him, a quiet movement, and a long stopping, and another slow drag or crawl. His throat contracted as he prepared to make the coyote howl of warning, but he waited for the next slow glide—surely a skulking Crow horse raider. It came, and Lance threw back his head and gave the high, thin cry of a coyote on a ridge in the night. There was a moment of silence and then a reply from another ridge, the sudden plunge of horses, two shots that were bright streaks of light, a shout of warning and silence except for the far running of the herd. A raider slipped past Lance and down the slope. Without thinking, he started after the man, trying to move only when he moved, and cautious of ambush.

Someone among the Sioux on the ridge called Lance back. There was a loud owl's hoot that could not be denied, and slowly he gave up just as three riders came whipping past him and away. On the ridge he discovered that the raiders had been driven off without getting any of the horses, but they had been very close when Lance gave the coyote howl of warning.

The herders brought the horses back and felt easier when a small party of warriors came up to ask about the shooting. The day herders arrived after dawn, and Lance started back to the camp. On the way down out of the hills he noticed the track of a small moccasin in the fresh earth of a pocket gopher pile. He leaned from his buckskin and then got down. It was certainly fresh, made during the night. The raiding Crows must have had a very small one along, much too small for the danger. Lance looked around for more tracks, found one in soft ground and then another, lower down, all heading up toward the herd. Curious, he looked along the dim trail and saw something bright in the grass—a red color stick. The color stick he had given to the little Ree.

Whirling his horse, he followed the tracks back up the hill toward the herding ground. They were harder to see on the well-grassed slopes but near the top he found more small moccasin prints, from wandering, weary feet. Then there were the narrow hoof marks of a mule, and suddenly no more of the small moccasins.

The little Ree was gone.

6 / The Cloudburst

It seemed the small Ree had been captured, probably by the Crows, those distant relatives and long-time enemies of the Sioux. Although it might have been someone from Sun Shield's village who picked up the boy wandering on the night prairie, the mule tracks did not lead toward his camp or any other Sioux village that Lance knew. Besides, none of the scouts or night herders had a mule. They were scarce and usually bought by the headmen for their women because mules were smart enough to smell out any danger, from rattlesnake to mountain lion. They never stepped foolishly into snow-covered washouts and couldn't be whipped into quicksand.

The leader of the night guard motioned to Lance impatiently. It was time to go in with the rest. The youth waved them on, leaning over his buckskin to search out the mule trail. Perhaps thinking that Lance had forgotten something on the herd ground, the man went on, down toward the village.

The mule tracks led Lance up the grassy slope, around through a draw, over the next ridge and down to a brushy little creek with a thread of water. In a clump of scrubby trees were signs of at least fifteen men hidden, close together, the horse droppings still soft and green inside. He found only two small moccasin tracks but considerable bloody sand where a wounded man, a big man, had lain a while and then rode on or was carried away. So the shooting at the herd had hit! Lance thought of something else: if the hurt man died, the little Ree would surely die too in a foolish avenging, his small body thrown out upon the prairie, bristling with arrows like a spiny cactus.

That was what impulsiveness could bring upon others, upon a small boy, Lance had to realize. What his string of impulsive acts, with no consideration for anyone else, could bring upon a helpless small boy.

But there was no time for regrets now. From here the trail would be very dangerous. The enemies, certain the Sioux would come to rescue the little captive, would surely prepare ambushes all along their hidden trail. Lance knew he should go to the village council, say what he had found, wait for a strong war party—and no telling what could happen to a little Ree boy by then.

Hurriedly Lance sliced the bark from the largest of the few trees, enough for a picture made with the red color stick, showing many pony tracks and one mule's, a boy with the Ree sign above him, and a Sioux following, identified by a lone lance. Then with only his bow and knife, not even a chunk of *wasna* in his pouch, he put the buckskin on the trail, but moving cautiously, afraid of an ambush anywhere, afraid he would see a small body dropped in the pursuer's path.

Lance tried to avoid the expected—the usual crawl to the top of every ridge, the travel just below the top, like the wolf, quick to dodge out of sight on either side. Instead, he dobbed his buckskin with mud from buffalo wallows that would dry gray as the sage and the barren earth of gully and draw. But he did crawl to an occasional high point to look around, and saw smoke signals from his village ordering him back. Someone had followed him to the enemy campground. At least it was known what had happened, where he had gone, and that the Ree boy was captured. He didn't stop or turn around and before long he saw a party of ten or fifteen on his trail, with horses he recognized from far off.

Now he was trapped between friends and enemies, both against his plans. Then he saw something those following couldn't know—that a large camp of Indians was moving in from across the river, visible only a moment, but visible. Lance jumped from his horse and left the signs "one hundred enemies ahead" on a bleached buffalo skull and laid it deliberately across his trail. But this knowledge didn't stop him; he merely turned scout, watcher, hoping for an opportunity to locate the little Ree whom the Crows evidently didn't intend to kill, at least not until he had tolled many Sioux under the sharp scalp knives.

By now the sun was disappearing into a cloud bank, with spring lightning like eyeblinks on the western horizon. Lance was hungry and gaunt-bellied, but there was no time for hunting now. He must find the Crow camp, study it, and without being caught. He thought the Sioux chasing him had given up until he saw a thin column of smoke signals, still calling him back, promising a real pipe-carried war to avenge the insult and the wrong.

Lance knew he should obey, that the good of the people must come first in any decision. So the infant had his birth cries choked off until he learned the silence that would never betray his village to skulking enemies. From birth to death, the people must come first. Yet the little Ree was his adopted brother; by bringing the captive home he had accepted the responsibility for his safety, his growth into manhood.

Turning his face westward, Lance kicked the weary buckskin along the shadowing slopes, looking for a place to hide her. The best was either a brush patch out on an open flat or a deep washout with barely room for the horse to move, even with the forelegs hobbled, but the washout lay in broken hills and would be easier to reach undetected in daylight if he had to make a run for it.

Lance pulled an armful of grass for the weary buckskin, loosened the jaw rope and tied it around his waist for any Crow horse he might catch. Cautiously he moved out upon the dusky prairie that seemed empty to ear and eye. Before sunset he had crept to a high point to study the thinning waterways ahead for a likely camping place to hold the large party. It must be off northwest and if no scout had detected him by now, Lance was certain he could locate the Crows by firelight or scent of smoke even in the coming storm, for surely so many had no need to hide.

The hunger gnawed so hard that the youth scarcely thought about his stiff knee as he slipped along the cuts and draws. There would be a late moon if the storm passed in time, and perhaps he could catch a rabbit, to be eaten raw, no matter how much he disliked raw meat. He moved faster as the darkness deepened, flowing his weight into his good leg much as a snake moves, silently. He kept sniffing the wind, but it was still in the east, blowing into the rising storm, and he was dependent upon his ears, hoping to catch the sound of a horse moving somewhere. By now he was going down a slope, with less smell of sagebrush against his leggings, more rooted sod under his moccasins. He put his ear to the ground and felt the movement of some animal, animals, starting, stopping, lighter-footed than horses, probably deer or antelope feeding. He must not rouse them by movement or man scent, not send them leaping away for any scout to hear.

The thunder rumbled closer and the lightning flung its

dangerous gleam over all the prairie. In one of these flashes he saw a rabbit feeding just ahead of him, nibbling hurriedly before the rain and wind. Lance drew his bow in the dark and, rising a little to see, waited for the next flicker of light. It came, and as he drew the arrow back, something dark fell over him—a robe. He struggled, but strong arms held him, took his bow and knife, twisted his wrists into a rawhide strip before him, and tied his ankles into a sort of hobble, like his horse. Suddenly a deep shame flooded over the young Sioux, even in this danger. Through his foolish impulsiveness the faithful buckskin was to die of thirst in the hidden draw, but the next bolt of lightning stopped this concern. Three men were riding down a canyon, one of them leading the buckskin horse. The bolt was very bright and left the image of his captors on the eyes of Lance for a long time—strong shiny brown faces, topped by upstanding rushes of hair, the Crow roach.

Hopelessly Lance got on his weary horse and let his feet be tied by rawhide strips under the buckskin belly. Then he was motioned into the middle of the little string of riders headed toward the storm-lit west. Over the next ridge the lightning showed a little valley, round as a shield, with a line of brush through the center. On the far side there was a cluster of low tipis and wickiups large enough for at least seventy, eighty warriors, with surely women along too, women who would care for the frightened Ree. Or was the boy frightened? Perhaps, if he was still alive, he was already the brother of the man who picked him up last night. But not if the Crow wounded in the horse herd had died. Each year or so some of the Oglala warriors and horse raiders who went against the Crows had to be keened, perhaps their bodies not recovered until long afterward. If important Crows were killed in the fighting, the dead Sioux might be hacked to pieces by the bereaved women.

Little Raven, the Crow who lived among the Sioux since

his capture up on the Tongue River long ago, laughed at these stories. "It is always the enemy who does these things. When I was a boy I heard it was the Sioux who chopped up the bodies of the dead left behind."

These stories came back to Lance now as he rode through the sheets of dry lightning and the shake and roar of thunder. His captors took him past the guarding scouts, through the quiet camp to the tipi of the headmen, a faint glow from the dying coals touching only their noses and their roaches of hair in the darkness.

The men looked over their pipes a long time. "A boy—!" one of them said at last, and started a murmur of talk in words that sounded familiar but only now and then with meaning. Lance held himself to silence against all questions, anxious to give them nothing that could put anyone to harm. Finally they brought in the frightened and sleepy little Ree. One of the men drew the boy's hands from his face and pointed to the prisoner in the firelight. A moment the boy stared. Then he tried to jump forward.

"My brother has come!" he cried, striking out at those who held him as he had struck at Lance, back on that first day, but then there had been a knife in his hand.

"Little brother," Lance said sharply, "we are captives!"

The little Ree looked puzzled for a moment at this new meaning for a word applied only to him for so many moons. Then his face became as stony as the day Lance found him, and remained so as they took him away. Later a woman brought meat for the scouts with Lance and put a piece of cool roasted deer into his tied hands. Without a knife he had to gnaw the meat, biting off huge mouthfuls, and as his hunger quieted, his hopelessness quieted a little too, and after a while he slept, waking at the sound of men riding in or out, listening each time for more captive Sioux or for words and signs of fighting. Each time he sank back into the cramped sleep of the bound man. The storm passed overhead, leaving the smell of lightning and of dust stirred by wind and the earth-shaking thunder.

Before dawn Lance was awakened to the sounds of a camp moving and was hurried to his horse. He couldn't see the Ree boy and hoped that he was alive and safe somewhere on one of the travois. They crossed the North Platte River at a wide, sandy-bottomed place above the Laramie, made a little hunt for meat and camped for the cooking.

Lance watched the horizon with special uneasiness, afraid of a Sioux attack—not fearing the certain cross fire so much as the enemy avenging if any Crows were killed. Perhaps to save the boy he should tell that he was a Ree, but then the little captive might be sent north, be traded off to friends up there.

Lance couldn't endure sitting around with his hands and feet tied to a cramping. There were only two women for all the work of the large party and so, by signs, he offered to help with the wood and the water if his hands were freed, his feet tied in walking hobbles. This seemed safe enough for a crippled youth, and afterward Lance sat to rest and made pictures with a weed stalk in the dust to amuse the easy-laughing little Crow boy along. Several of the men gathered around to watch him draw a line of straight-sitting riders with high roaches, the tails of their horses tied up in the sign of war.

One of the women brought out a skin and asked Lance to copy the dust picture upon it. He signed an apology that he had nothing except the charcoal from the fire because his only color stick had been taken from him. The woman smiled her understanding, her handsome white teeth gleaming, and so Lance drew the picture for her and added a fine Crow parading around the outside, the lances all flying scalps that looked like the tufts of horse hair that they usually were. He added a picture of the small boy too, with the upstanding brush at the forehead. The woman brought the little Ree to see it with her son, making motions of cutting the Ree's hair into a roach too, and laughed at his face, suddenly hard and stubborn against her.

When the skin was done Lance made more sketches in the dust, amusing little lines that were a moccasin, an ax, and a bear cub, all pictures standing for the names of his relatives and people at the lodge where the Ree had lived among the Sioux. He explained to the boys how one showed a flight of arrows by a line of them going out, or gunshots by puffs of flying powder, and the movement of people by many pony tracks going in the same direction.

"Try making signs," he said, "make the signs in the dirt."

The Crow son tried earnestly, drawing the sign for his tribe, a crow flying, and a very good and recognizable crow it was. The Ree stared at the boy's finger moving easily in the dust and started a picture himself, but at an angry word from one of the men, the woman came to take the little captive away, and so quickly that Lance could not be certain if the boy understood his meaning, or if the man suspected it.

From the impatient loafing, the slow moves, Lance was sure that his captors were waiting for something, for scout word of buffaloes or enemies or perhaps for another party of warriors to attack the Sioux villages in the region. He must try to get the little Ree away before that. He could probably escape his rawhide bindings in the night but he must know where the boy slept. To make the attempt and fail would only bring a Crow knife to his throat.

Evenings men came in, and went out in the darkness, war men. Lance, increasingly uneasy, tried to sneak some good glances around while he carried water from the creek for the morning fires, plodding as slowly in the galling thongs as he dared. He knew there was another storm on the way, perhaps more thunder and dust, although this time the birds flew up with a curious haste and flutter of excitement, the few horses kept picketed in the camp stamping aimlessly. Several times he saw the Crow boy ride out behind his father, clinging to the man's rawhide belt, but there was no sign of the little Ree. Some days later, perhaps because they were far from the Sioux villages, the captive boy was permitted a lonely playing. He wandered about, throwing pebbles ahead of him at imagined rabbits and birds. Several times he sat down to gather up another handful of stones, taking long at it, moving a finger in the dust, or so Lance hoped.

Then one day, when the sun was high as the shoulder, the camp was suddenly ordered to move. It wasn't like the other times. Today the warriors painted themselves carefully, not as for war, more for adornment, for a visiting and dance time. The two women put on handsome red-flannel dresses, with thick ropes of necklaces on their breasts, their faces ochered, the vermilion bright on the cheeks. They brought out beaded trappings for their horses, the fringes almost to the ground, their saddle and saddlebags crusted in beadwork. Even the little Ree was given a few adorning swipes of paint, and a shirt quickly made from a painted buckskin sack. Then they started in slow formal march over a ridge and into a narrow green valley with a sparkling creek flowing over rocks. Around a bend Lance saw a large Crow village of at least two hundred lodges, perhaps the entire tribe. The camp stretched along the narrow strip of bottom between the swift stream and the high bluffs that reached up to a wide grassy plain—a fine place for a buffalo drive over the steep bluff walls. The herds of horses grazing on the high prairie were so many they seemed dark as a feeding buffalo herd that feared no enemy.

The newcomers, with the captives, were sent on up the creek. They settled on the narrow slope between the bluffs and the stream—the only campground left in the pleasant little valley. Before the small shelters were up, visitors came from the big camp for a friendly smoke and a look at the two captives. The war leaders walked around Lance, talking among themselves and examining him from all sides as one would an unusual horse from the Nez Percé country. The medicine healer motioned Lance to sit down, to stretch out his bad leg, and ran his long fingers over and under the wounded knee, searching out the tender spots, pressing hard, watching the movement of the flesh for signs of pain that the youth would not betray. The man said something to the others and motioned Lance to rise. He stood, holding himself as straight and proud as possible in the thongs, as a Sioux must before such bold enemies of his people.

The visitors looked at the little Ree too, with the open faces of Indians for children. The boy, after six moons of kindness, showed almost none of the animal fear Lance had found in him last fall, a small shivering and starving animal in the place where his relatives had been killed. The medicine man thumped the boy's back, put his head under the shoulder blade, looked into the lifted eyelid and grunted his approval.

After dark the Crow camps danced their victories together—two captives and three fresh Sioux scalps. Lance was on the ground and couldn't see or hear much but the drumming, the yells and singing that went on a long, long time. He tried to catch a word or a name to locate the fight, identify those killed, or see the scalp locks for some recognizable feather, bead, or stone still tied to the hair. As the excitement rose and the daring and the threats, he began to fear for the little Ree and for himself, wondering if some important Crow had been brought down in the fighting, determined if it came to violence, to shout out the boy's tribe.

The far lightning grew and a little thunder began to rumble, in the northeast this time, a sign that this storm would not be a dry one. With the great fires blazing and the wild dancing, the crowd paid no attention until a patter of rain swept over them and grew thicker, until the flames sputtered and fried and began to blacken. Dancers backed out of the circling as the rain struck harder, stumbling in the darkness until finally even the scalp takers and their women started to run in the driving sheets of water.

Someone remembered Lance and felt around for him. One of the men stumbled over his legs in the wet grass. Something slipped down to the youth's side—a knife, from the Crow's sheath. Lance worked his bound hands around and pushed the knife under the belt of his breechclout, hoping it would stay as he was jerked up and led hobbling to the camp on the slope, peering into the driving rain, trying by the pale, far-off lightning to see where the women took the Ree.

Although the storm roared like hail up on the high table above the bluffs, it slacked to a steady patter as the wet camp settled into a cold and weary sleep. With two men in the wickiup, Lance had to be very careful as he worked the knife in his belt around behind him and tried to saw at the thongs of his wrists. Once the men beside him stirred, but he lay still as they grumbled, apparently at the cold rain soaking in. Finally he had his hands free and reached as cautiously as a snake on a birdling toward the hobbles and cut them.

Afterward he held himself to the slow shallow breath of sleep, trying to plan a way out of the wickiup and to the Ree. But a rumbling rose in his ear against the ground, not broken as thunder was, but steady, as of a buffalo stampede sweeping in from the prairie above the camp. Then there were horses running, shouts of warning, and cries along the slope, lost in the rising thunder and roar as the icy wall of a cloudburst struck Lance's wickiup and swept everything away in a churning of water, earth, rock, wood, brush and moving creatures—horses and people.

Lance fought to get out, was hit on the head by a log or rock or hoof and went down, and dragged himself up again, choking, coughing, his lungs full of muddy water. In the darkness he tried to swim sideways to the flood, powerful as ever, but clearer now of rolling rocks and earth. Suddenly his good foot found bottom and he began to shout as everyone else, all far away by now, it seemed. But he was shouting "Little Ree, where are you?" forgetting his captors and that they were Crows, forgetting everything except that a small boy was in that roaring flood somewhere. He tried to brace himself against the force of the waters, waiting for lightning, for any sight or sound except the roaring and the darkness. Overhead the clouds were solid, the faint flashes trapped high up as the storm moved on, but the water still poured down the bluff slope, even deepening in the blackness of the night, the cries spreading down the valley, to be lost in the thunder of water.

Then Lance thought he heard Sioux words above the noise, not only Siouxlike Crow speech, but pure Sioux.

"Where are you?" the words called out, and were followed by the momentary spark of a knife struck on dry flintstone.

Lance was afraid to believe his ears or his eyes, and afraid to answer, with Crows surely still around. Cautiously he fought the flood toward what seemed higher ground. Once he went under and was swept down, to lodge in a great pile of brush and weeds, with something, some creature, struggling in it. He swam away through the water curling around the pile, touched bottom and began to push his way outward again where he remembered a low ridge. He tried shouting some wordless sounds and waited. Someone or something seemed to be working toward him. He braced his good leg against the push of the water, remembered his knife and clutched it, ready. Cautiously he crouched down to catch anything above him against the sky if lightning came again. There was a far flicker, and then another, also faint, but they showed two men on horses at the rim of the bluffs and what looked like more riders farther off—Crow scouts or at least someone who spoke Sioux. He heard horses move, perhaps upon him, perhaps to get out of sight of any gun-armed men below. There was another call, plain this time in the slackening noise. "Lance! Lance! Where are you?"

It was the roaring voice of Jumping Moose, come to find his young scout after another foolish act.

Lance gave his owl hoot, thrown away, to seem to come from another place, and started toward the bluff. Then he remembered the little Ree. It would be unbelievable luck to find him alive, in addition to the Sioux coming, but it must happen. Without the boy he could not go back, no matter how impossible the finding seemed. In a desperate moment of daring, Lance turned his eyes to the black sky, to the place where the earth was and around the four great directions. "Help me!" he cried within himself. "Help me and I will take part in the sun dance if the boy can be saved. I will dance facing the sun all the four holy days—"

Then the young Sioux realized what he had done, and became afraid. He was not worthy of a vow, had no right to make it to save himself or anyone from his foolish deeds. Such things were only for grown men working for the good of the people. Yet he could not retract the vow now, would not if he could. He would make the dance.

Slowly, carefully, Lance worked his way to the Sioux, hidden but still at the edge of the slope. It was good that Lance was safe, Jumping Moose whispered, but they knew nothing of the little Ree. The boy must be here. The pictures they had followed in the dust carried the mark of a small corn sheller, a small Ree. That was how they found the right camp.

A flood of gratitude to the boy swept over Lance, to the one still to be found although there were two hundred Crow warriors down there in the darkness and even if it was only a drowned little body.

Jumping Moose led the way along the torn slope, climbing through washouts, keeping just below the top, seeing very much with his trained night eyes. By now the flood was only small streamlets and gurglings under the far cries of the people and the keening of the Crow women down the creek.

They found more of the Sioux party, two of them with a captured Crow woman from the big camp. There were the sounds of many searchers coming up the flooded little valley, making it dangerous for fifteen Sioux. Besides, the little whitening in the eastern clouds spoke of the dawn to come. The men tried to talk to the Crow captive by signs in the darkness, but she stood silent.

Lance went back to the little camp ground, the whole slope washed and water-gutted, the ground slippery as bear grease. Down near the creek he felt around over the piles of trash for bodies and found two grown Indians, a horse, and some furry creatures wet and sad to the touch. He tried to think—make himself a small boy, unshackled, but surely tied to something, perhaps a tipi pin. What would he have grabbed for in the flood—one of the women, a tipi pole, or the rope that tied him?

Then something occurred to Lance. There had been a large old log near the far end of the camp, perhaps too well settled into the earth for the shallower edge of the flood. He worked his way carefully because by now the rattlesnakes, washed out, would be warming and fighting mad. He hurried and was stopped by the squashy footsteps of a large party of Crows coming up the slope, apparently moving in a wide row, searching the ground for the wounded and the dead. There was a shout when they found the bodies in the pile of brush, and then more steady walking, and some talk too, the men apparently unaware that there might be Sioux around. Lance listened for any names of survivors from the camp here—the little Ree or the pleasant woman who was kind to him, but the words seemed mostly of the disastrous cloudburst, and as Lance finally realized, of their two captives.

So the little Ree hadn't been found either, dead or alive.

Lance started to slip away, but more Crows coming along the slope had him cut off, and he found himself walking in the long dark row that moved up through the camp ground. He stepped and stumbled with the men in the darkness. When they reached the top of the slope they divided and went down the edges of the camp, moving more carefully downhill, feeling out everything. It was then that Lance slipped into a deep washout at the end of the old log he had sought. Those beside him pushed up close to help, but he grunted and climbed out alone and walked firmly on, looking for a place to escape now, to slip away unnoticed before any observed the limp that he tried to hide. At the big pile of trash, wickiups, tipis, and mud caught in a clump of brush, they found another body. Lance helped lift it out and then pawed around seeming to hunt for more. Actually he crawled down under the tangle of poles and tipi robes. The searchers with the dead man called to the others, and finally the party re-formed below the tangle and went on toward the creek.

When they seemed gone, Lance slipped back to the washout and dropped down into it, feeling around in the cutback. There was only earth and mud, but when he ran his hand over the wet ground a second time it felt warmish to the palm, with a hole behind it, apparently dug out since the flood. He backed away, out of easy reach of any hiding

Crow and whispered, "Little Ree—little brother—"

At first there was no sound or movement, but when he whispered again, "It is Lance!" there was a stirring back in the darkness and the boy crawled out. He was still cautious but wet and shaking. The first rush of water had washed out the picket pin he was tied to. With nobody around to grab him, he tucked the rope around his waist and tried to get to the edge of the flood. He found the old log, clung to it, and when the waters quieted, hid in the washout.

Lance lifted the boy out. Stealthily but as fast as possible they climbed up to Jumping Moose. He was very impatient, with so much shouting and hurry coming from the big camp below. Trouble was close. While they doubled Lance and the Ree on horses behind the warriors a red shot whistled past them, with shouting, and two more bullets flying over their heads.

The Sioux kicked their heels into the ribs of their horses and were gone, throwing mud, but it was a good thing that the Crow herds were scattered or they would have had a long fight getting home. As it was, they rode hard, and when day rose along the east, Lance was filled with thankfulness to the storm and the cloudburst and the noble red sky from which they came.

Then he remembered something: his vow for the sun dance.

7 / Sun Dance and Bear Butte

BY THE TIME Lance and the little Ree were back from Crow captivity, the trading was done and the parfleches empty of meat, without one buffalo bull pawing the spring earth anywhere along the Platte, not one yellow calf bucking and playing with the vagrant little whirlwinds running in the dust. Instead, the dark moving figures in the valley were long strings of white men hurrying up the river trail, their far-shooting guns killing and scaring the game, their horses and bull teams eating the grass as it looked out of the ground, and dirtying the streams. Not long ago, just before Lance made his puberty dreaming, the Platte valley had stood belly-deep in grass to their horses, and now the ground was bare as an old dance spot.

There was a growing anger against the whites, particularly among the young warriors, who had to see the bleaching bones of their buffaloes, and the wagons passing with valuable guns and all the unknown wonderful things hidden in those wickiups on wheels. Many from the Loaf About the Forts went to the camps of the freighters and emigrants, begging or demanding something for their grass gone and their game. Sometimes they were given a little tobacco and coffee but often they were driven away, even shot at, but no one must shoot back. Even when the Indians kept the peace the soldiers always came riding up the trail. The white soldier chief usually called the headmen of the Indians together and demanded that they keep away from the trail.

"Go up to the Tongue and the Yellowstone country," he would order. "Keep your warriors out of the valley of the Platte."

This year Lance had been among those who rode over to see this white soldier chief make the big talk. He saw the anger in Sun Shield and the rest at this man who came to tell them where to go in their own country. It was the white man who should keep away from the Indian's river. But the soldiers had many guns, some the big ones on wheels, like wagons, guns that threw balls as big as the buffalo bull bladders—bigger even—heavy black iron balls that burst and blew the tops off small hills and tore up anything in their path. After the echoes died, the smoke spread, and the frightened women and children stopped running.

So Sun Shield's village moved to the Tongue River, up near the mouth. They had relatives among the band of Oglala Sioux who lived in that region from the old, old days, before any grandmother could remember, and they were friends with the Northern Cheyennes up there too. Besides, the scouts reported buffalo on the Tongue, and the Indians had to go where they could make meat.

Because Lance had got three buffaloes in the hunt last fall, he was sent out with the meat men ahead of the moving village. They found a scattering of the animals all the way north from the head of the Powder River. Lance felt good. The loafing around, hobbled, in the Crow camp had helped the last healing under his knee, and his careful working—bending it a little farther every day, no matter how much it hurt—had brought some of the limberness back. He could walk without limping at all if he was careful, enough so that the warrior society of his father's youth was inviting him to their lodge again, although he still did not go very often where the talk was all about coups and scalps, war booty and pretty girls.

"You will have to learn to work with a party, not sneak off alone," the young war chief of the society told him, and planned some team games for him, and relay horse races and wrestling matches. Somehow Lance was gone before the plans were completed. Deer Foot had seen him slip out under the lodge flaps and followed.

"Do not be foolish, my friend," he advised, with the formality of one who was now a warrior too.

But when Lance made no reply, the Deer became sad. "Once we were friends like twin colts running together, and Cedar too. You always the leader, a step ahead. You have hunted and killed and captured, but we are the ones who are sung out of the village by the young women."

Still Lance kept walking, with no words.

"Think of your father, one of the Shirtwearers, the most honored of all the Sioux!"

"That is for wisdom and justice and humility," Lance defended.

"And the bearing of the holy lances into battle?"

To this there was no defense except anger. "They have told you what to say to me!" Lance accused, and with this he was gone between the dark lodges, running into the hills.

Lance could join in the dances again. He discovered this at the celebration after the cloudburst. The crier had run through the village with invitation sticks for Lance and the little Ree to come to eat here, eat there, until the boy looked as stuffed as a bear cub ready for the winter's sleep—more like a little bear than his adopted twin, the taller and somewhat older Cub. At the lodge of Blue Dawn the girl put the bowls of meat into the hands of the guests herself, and hovered over them, saying: "Eat! Eat! We are made proud!"

Later there was the dancing for the victories, the young Crow woman standing handsomely painted and dressed by the family of her captor, and much haranguing and rejoicing over the two rescued from the enemy, from the shadow of the death scaffold. In the dances Dawn had drawn Lance back to her each time that another girl circled the fire with him, even if it was her friend Shying Leaf. Finally the young Sioux was breathless and laughing, and aware that he had forgotten his bad knee, the knee that was hardly bad any more.

The village camped on a broad valley of the Tongue, preparing for the sun dance, which was to come when the sun seemed highest. There was much new country to look over, and much visiting around their northern friends and their trading posts, and much racing and horse swapping, and many small raids against the herds of the Crows and the Snakes. Lance spent most of his time preparing for the sun dance. There was some smoking and talk about his participation by the advisers, and some doubt. It was not common for one so young to dance the sun, certainly not for a personal favor instead of something to save the people. Still, all vows must be fulfilled if there was not to be a sorrow or a loss upon perhaps all the village.

While he waited Lance went to sit on a bluff overlooking his camp, all his people, and thought about his duty to the Powers that encompassed all the earth and the sky. His plea had been heard in the midst of the cloudburst, but somehow what had seemed so clearly right then was like a paling dream now—the storm, his sense of a great oneness with all the things. Or was it only because he wanted to avoid the results of his foolishness?

To see what had been done more clearly he started to make sketches in the dust and feeling that he needed something more permanent, he went down to his second mother to beg odd pieces of buckskin for his pictures. Feather Woman looked up from her beading for a long time and then sent him to the wife of old Paint Maker, the man who kept the history of the Sun Shield band. "She knows the good way to make the skins—"

Lance was ashamed to approach this tall, quiet-spoken woman of the picture man's lodge, always busy with the ceremonials and the tanning.

"You shall have the choice of my next horse catchings," he offered, awkward as a boy.

"A good steady mare to drag the lodge poles would be appreciated," the Paint Maker's wife said, smiling a little, knowing how uninterested the young Sioux, even the girls, were in such tame animals. She brought out an armful of skin pieces, some no larger than the hand, some big as the side of an antelope. "Perhaps you can use five or six of the best. They are a poor enough gift."

"I shall tell Feather Woman of your kindness," he said, in the indirect way of the Sioux.

Now he set to work, drawing with charcoal and the color sticks, rubbing out mistakes with the wetted root of the soap weed and redrawing when the skin dried. He hoped to tell the whole story from the day he found the little Ree and all he had done since, all that had happened, mostly events that no one could tell for him as was done for war honors, where others saw and helped. He tried to put in something of his feeling when he made the vow in the darkness where the water had roared over the bluffs like the falls of the Yellowstone. Yet he had vowed for no one except the Ree, his captive, who was his own responsibility.

Uneasily Lance finished the pictures that he wished to take to the holy man, the adviser of his puberty fastings.

He and the others must be convinced that the one who had been given the grown-up name of Lone Lance by his father's song through the village was truly a man, a man who could make a proper vow. Otherwise, he would not be permitted in the sun dance, and his promise would be no more than a child's boast on the wind.

Finally, Lance had to go down into the village where the councilors sat at their evening circle, smoking, planning the management of the sun-dance time. Good Axe, under the privilege of his honors, took the roll of pictures to the adviser.

"It is asked that you consider the things shown here and remember the Ree brought in, the eagle captured alone, the sweet meat of his three buffaloes, his scouting the Crows, and how he was at Crow Butte and in the drunken Loafer camp and now in the cloudburst."

The holy man tamped his pipe with his thumb, guttered the stem in the silence, and let the bundle be laid before him.

That evening the village was quiet, with many of the young people preparing for their part in the sun-dance preliminaries. Very few knew which maidens were selected to go out with the holy man to pick the *wakan* tree, the center pole for the sun dance, but many thought that Blue Dawn would be among the four. Lance heard these whispers with pride and looked toward his twin sisters, soon of the age too, but mostly he was concerned about the decision of the advisers tomorrow.

The sun came up clear and hot, but Lance could not go to the horse herds, or with the hunters, not even with the bathers to the swift clear waters of the Tongue. Only the small ones were playing—Cub and the little Ree with other boys, running over the prairie like spring colts, but away from the serene quietness of the village. Moccasin and

Feather Woman were out near them, gathering the sacred white sage to spread over the proper places. They piled it on robes until they had made high whitish knolls and then the helpers came to bear the sage back in a little procession.

When the two men with the escorting staffs finally came for Lance, waiting at his mother's lodge, it seemed that his knees were suddenly broken, both of them. He managed to rise, walk between the silent escorts and stoop through the lodge door, to stand until the man at the far side lifted his dark and shriveled face, looked around the others, and motioned the escorts away.

It was shadowed evening when Lance stumbled out of the lodge of the advisers. He had been inside since the sun was overhead and he recalled nothing of it except, as in a dreaming, he learned that he was not yet a man fit to dance a vow. Next year, perhaps, or later, but not this summer.

As one empty of all worth, he walked across the village circle, not permitting himself to slip around behind the lodges, out of sight. Deer Foot motioned to him quietly, wanting to know. Cub and the little Ree started to run toward him, and were waved back by the men, to stand with blank, uncomprehending faces, the Cub pulling at one of his growing braids.

Lance knew he would be watched to keep him from what the holy man called more of his thoughtless and impulsive ventures that endangered everybody. It would be particularly dangerous up here, this running out alone, with so many enemies around: Crows, Snakes, Gros Ventres, Assiniboines, and the far-ranging Blackfeet.

But because it was not good to have a disappointed vower in the sun-dance village, he was advised to go to help around the farthest horse herds. He gathered up his sleeping robe, rode out behind one of the night guards and stayed up there, out of sight of the river and the village. Food was sent to him, and coffee, and once raisins, fresh from the trader. The little Ree came too, with Cub, the boys clinging behind the herders. They ate up the raisins while they looked at the pictures Lance had drawn, those he wanted other eyes to see.

When the half-moon time of the ceremonials ended and the last drumming, the last song, was dead on the wind, the youth returned home. He rode in past the dance place: the circle arbor covered with pine boughs browning; the sun-dance pole in the center bare and forgotten, the colored streamers, the feathers and symbolic figures of man and buffalo once tied to the top all gone. The grass of the place was worn and blown away, the willow arches of the sweat lodge like thin, empty ribs open to the sky.

At the village the buffalo scouts were out, the people ready for a rapid move at the first signal. Twice the signals came but spoke only of small bunches seen, not the great herd a good sun dance was to bring. Each time the village moved eastward a little. Once they stopped to wait until their friends, the Cheyennes, had made an antelope drive into their ancient pits. It was not the best season, but the Old Ones saw a hard winter ahead, one to eat up all the dried meat anyone could make. Perhaps the same warning caused the unusual bunchings of the lithe, handsome animals moving over the prairie.

Lance went with a small party of young Sioux to help with the drive.

"It is good to have seen this done once," Moccasin had agreed.

They got to the Cheyennes the day before the drive and were given tentative locations for their hiding on the long path to the pits, the exact spots depending upon where the little bunches of antelope were and the wind direction. For three days the clouds had run over the grass tops, but the morning after the visitors arrived the sun burned the sky as clear as the blue of a Sioux woman's beaded yoke. The hunters from far out started the drive, whooping the shying antelope together, the white of their rumps plain as they fled, only to be turned back upon themselves by other bunches fleeing from other whooping, robe-waving riders. Slowly they were pushed together, more waiting horsemen charging out at one side and then the other. As the shouts and man-smell neared from both sides, and behind, the animals became frantic, confused, running this way and that, the young and the weak forgotten, trampled, left behind in the dust.

By now the herd brought together could run in only one direction, with more men and women and children rising up to flap skins and shout, narrowing the escape path until suddenly the antelope were running between new brush fences. They threw themselves against these, and were sent back by more whoops and man-smell, springing up behind the brushy walls that drew closer and closer together until the antelope were forced along in a solid stream of wild, plunging creatures. The slender heads, the delicate black-and-white throats of the elegant pronghorns hurling themselves desperately together and apart made a silent crying in the breast of Lance. As the drivers whooped louder, closer, the panic in the herd increased, and the surge forward, until the stronger ones ahead saw the ground suddenly gone before their feet—nothing but the wide-open pit ahead. They tried to leap it and fell, those behind pouring over them, the cries of the wounded animals lost in the triumphant shouts of the hunters. Only one antelope managed to break back from the very hole, to dodge under the horses and between them and away. No one pursued him, not a creature of such courage.

At the pit the meat men plunged in with clubs and knives, killing and piling the dead aside, until the last beautiful, broken body ceased to struggle, the last frantic leg to spring. Then the women ran in for the butchering.

Lance had helped with the hunt but he could not bear to see the antelope broken and killed this way—driven in panic to destroy themselves—the same beautiful ones that had come to stand beside his hole last winter, to accept his arrows, and to die gently so he could live.

Three days later Lance was with his village again, just too late to see the buffaloes stampeded over the bluffs at the creek to be called Cabin, the animals sent running much as the antelope were, but over steep cliffs not made by man.

The next half-moon was a busy time for the women, with good young meat to dry hard as wood in one hot, windy day, and many light robes to be stripped of their thin summer woolling for lodge skins and a hundred other uses. Lance grieved less over his unfulfilled vow. He danced the good hunts with the rest, first among the Cheyennes and then with the Sioux. Finally the lodge skins were ready to take from the curing water, the dry meat stored, the chokecherries picked and pounded with the roasted dried meat for the bladders of *wasna*. The camp circle was neat, the lodges for the council and the headmen newly painted. Then Sun Shield's village moved out with the Northern Oglalas and the other divisions of the western—the Teton—Sioux, toward their annual gathering at Bear Butte, the dark mountain of the crouching bear, up beyond *Pa Sapa*, the Black Hills.

This annual move to the great council was always the finest of the year. Lance, off on a rise with the horse herds, watched his village make ready for the trail as though he had never seen it before. He was no longer on his favorite buckskin, lost to the Crows in the Platte country, but rode a spotted black-and-white, gayer but not as trustworthy, and conspicuous to the eye of game or enemy from far off.

The broad summer valley below Lance was a fine pattern of color and movement. He could see some of the scouts far ahead and the out-guards two ridges beyond them, making the route safe. Down at the village the Dog Soldiers were lined up, waiting, by vow never to move until the last of the people were safely away from camp or from enemy attack. Perhaps it would be good to belong to this warrior society, but it was hard to become a Dog Soldier. One had to do very daring things in war. Sometimes, in a desperate fight, the young warrior set himself against any retreat by staking down the Dog rope he always wore tied to his waist. Then he could only advance, drive the enemy back or die fighting at his stake unless someone ran in to pull it up and rescue him. There were stories of warriors who left the Dog stake circled with dead enemies before they went down.

Lance knew that such men showed this boldness and bravery early in their boyhood. The Sioux killed trying to get up on Crow Butte had been found alive under two dead Pawnees, dead by his weapons, when he was only fifteen. Truly so long as the Dog Soldiers were strong the women and children knew there was a wall between them and any pursuing enemy.

As always, the first to start were fifteen or twenty warriors selected to ride out abreast, their horses red, black, gray, and golden today, with several white-patched as in summer snow. Even from far off Lance caught the sun glint on the heads of the feathered spears and knew the men had the painted shields at their sides, the ceremonial quivers and long bows on their backs. The leggings and breechclouts were certainly the finest, the shirts of the leaders beaded, fringed and soft. Others rode bare to the waist, painted, not for war but for the joy of the move, and all had the formal whitened robes folded across their horses before them.

After the line of warriors came the four old pipe-bearers, the oldest of the councilors, carrying their ancient pipes of red stone, the long stems and the beaded pipe bags decorated with flutterings of feather and fringe. They were followed by more warriors, with still others waiting in little groups to fall into place as the village lengthened along the valley. The families stood ready at their places in the camp circle, taking the same position in the moving column. Every wife rode in her handsomest array to show the position and affection of her husband, her saddle trappings rich in beading and fringe and flying bands of color. Many of the younger women wore the blue-beaded-yoke dresses, a few of the older in flannel, mostly dark blue, with perhaps hundreds of elk teeth in rows around the bosom and skirt.

At the knobs of the women's saddles hung the adorned cradleboards of the very young or the painted hide sacks for the newly walking ones, and for cherished small belongings. Behind each family walked the travois horses, dragging the lodge poles, the skins piled on top, others with the bed robes, the regalia, and people too, the old and weary, the ill and crippled. Sometimes there were willow baskets or cages for the children too big for the saddle bags and too young to cling behind some rider or on a horse alone, and for the kettles, bowls, and other small belongings that an upset or a runaway might lose in brush or tall grass.

At the sides of this moving village rode the young unmarried women and girls, dressed and painted in their best, the long bands of beads and white shell cores hanging from their shining braids. Around the outside of the whole column rode the boys and youths, showing off, singing or riding in headlong charges, perhaps touching their moccasin toes to the ground on one side and then the other or slipping down the tail of a galloping horse and springing back up, perhaps sliding through under the panting belly. The trilling cries of admiration rose from the girls, and perhaps a hurting laughter when a horse stepped into a badger hole, throwing the rider over his head into the dust, and a murmur of concern if, as seldom happened, the rider was injured.

Lance knew from his high hill that Blue Dawn would be riding among the young women now because she had been the leader of the four maidens selected for the sun dance which had brought such a rich harvest of summer meat and robes. Deer Foot would be showing off before her as a young warrior now, and Cedar there too, but riding in the dignity he felt was due the girl for whom warriors waited in their courting blankets outside the lodge door. Suddenly Lance was bitter with envy of Deer Foot, this friend of the brash daring, but he would not go down to ride with the other youths, and he was not a warrior.

Finally even the Dog Soldiers were moving along the timbered creek and up the divide, eastward. Pride filled the breast of Lance tight as a bale of robes. In his mind he drew the varying outlines of the moving camp, determined that he would picture it all on a skin during the half-moon's time at Bear Butte—a whole buffalo cow skin, if he could beg one from his relatives, half for the moving and the rest for the great annual council of the Teton Sioux, which he had not seen since he was old enough to understand. The last few years there was always some sickness. The little spotted disease called the measles that killed so many among some of the northern people had kept the cautious Sun Shield away for two meetings. Then the big stinking spotted disease, the smallpox, struck his village and sent so many to the death scaffold that there was no heart left for the council.

But now was a new time, with new things for the Sioux nation to consider. Lance knew a little about the problems for the great meeting, problems that had taken Good Axe around the other bands most of last spring. The white man was pushing in all along the east and breaking the Indian country in two by the Platte River trail, breaking it like a rock is broken. The grass was gone from that fine region, the buffaloes very scarce.

When the village was past, Lance touched his heel to his horse and, avoiding the dust blowing off to the side, he took his place with the youths racing along the edge of the moving camp, seeking out Blue Dawn. But he had to go help Old Grandmother, who had outlived all her relatives. One of her travois horses had shied at something, broken loose and headed for the open prairie, the poles bouncing their load. A lot of the young boys whooped after the mare, pretending they tried to catch her but really keeping her in a run. The men laughed and roared at the goods scattered on the wind, and the shouting anger of the old woman famous for her sharp tongue.

Four days later Lance was among the scouts far out ahead of the village. He stopped on a rise south of Bear Butte, a small mountain standing off alone, black as charcoal—a great black bear crouching, head down and always turned toward the rising sun. From between the bear's shoulders smoke rose in one tall straight feather to the sky, and spread there. This fire was always built by the first arrivals and kept burning night and day until the council was over and the last rear guard gone. Many times during the year there would be fires there, visible over wide prairies, signaling some message, some emergency to the tribe.

Below Lance the people were crossing the alkali flat with its white dust, and moving out upon the wide valley east of the Bear, under his strong look. They headed toward their place among the Oglalas, one of the seven divisions of the Teton Sioux, and all camped in one great circle here. It scarcely seemed possible that so many people lived on the earth, and their pony herds were like clouds over the low, rolling upland on both sides of the valley farther than anyone could see, making the rises as dark as the Black Hills standing against the southwestern sky. Lance had been to the Hills with small parties who went quietly, reverently, to stay a while in the cool, shaded canyons, to camp near the roaring waterfalls. Perhaps they stopped at the thick forests of slender pines for new lodge and travois poles. It was a holy place, for peace, but usually those who wanted special guidance for the people went on to fast at the butte that was a crouching bear and to light the fire in the protected place between the shoulders, where the smoke rose straight as a chief's feather.

When the scouts reached the vast Teton circle, the big council lodge was being set up in the center. Many painted skins were laced together and stretched over poles from the deepest canyons of the Black Hills, a lodge big as twenty put together, and standing tall as the pines. Here all the headmen of the Tetons would gather, the great Sioux pipe would be filled and the long smoke begun.

Everywhere there were special things to be seen, special honors to inspect and approve. As soon as his second mother had the lodge up she brought out the stand and the regalia of Moccasin: his feathered lance, his shield, the long-tailed warbonnet of his younger days, and the garments of his ceremonials. All around the great circle it was the same, the stands colorful with regalia, feathers blowing in the evening wind, drums and flutes and special medicine things. Here and there a few honored lodges had no regalia out, no display at all—the lodges of the holy ones and of headmen like Good Axe, made a Shirtwearer, and vowed to be poorer than the poorest among them.

Lance thought about his father's honors. Perhaps if he had tried to be a great warrior, he might have been asked to bear one of the sacred lances into battle someday, even be made a Shirtwearer. But these honors were for more than bravery in war, for judgment too, and for wisdom, vision, selflessness, and the great heart. In none of these could he ever hope to fill the moccasins of Good Axe—not with his scattering ways that concerned all his parents, many scattering paths, and self-willed on all of them.

The first few days in the great encampment were gay ones and busy too, keeping the herds of horses that darkened the far hills in grass and water, and from straying home to their own familiar range. The hunters were out several sleeps away, to get fresh meat for so many, and the wood and water haulers worked all day. But there was much fun for the young, the children running here and there with new companions to discover, to test out in games as young animals do in their running. There were boys' wrestling matches, foot races, and the stick and ring contests as hot as among the grown men. Youths gathered from different bands in the game of "Throwing Off the Horses." The riders formed two lines, facing, the sides distinguished perhaps by a swipe of clay or paint—White against Gray or whatever was available. With loud whoops the Indians charged straight together, the horses meeting shoulder against shoulder, rearing, floundering, some to go down in a tangle of kicking and dust, the youths grabbing for any opponent still mounted, to pull and jerk and wrestle him off his horse, until all the riders of one side were on the ground, called dead, as in war. Young boys played this game too, sometimes, stripped to breechclout and moccasins, as warriors went into battle. And if one fell backward into a cactus bed, it was very funny for all the others, all except the one who had to walk instead of ride for a while.

There were the big horse races too, with the bets piled at the foot of the wager posts, the horses whipped in, and wrestling and foot races for tribal championships, with the watchers spread like wide dark robes on all sides. There was walking along the water path and new matches made, perhaps from attractions at the last encampment, those that had endured the usual "winter of the waiting." In the evenings there were the great brush fires with drumming, songs and dances everywhere. Groups of young people visited from one band to another, and to the other divisions —Oglalas to the northern Hunkpapas, perhaps, and the Brules to the Sans Arcs, the No Bows, because they saw them only once a year and found all their accounts and exploits new and fine to know. As the young people went around the circle, more and more were drawn to join them until there was a great singing, laughing string moving past the hundreds of fires and thanking the older people who called out songs of praise, and of teasing, perhaps.

Once Lance was sent with the Oglala warriors to stand guard at the entrance of the large council lodge, the skins rolled up for air, the sight of the men in the circle inside awing the passersby. Lance held himself sternly straight at the entrance, within touching distance of the great ones of the Teton Sioux—the old-time warriors and the wise and holy ones, some from families known for generations for their important men and women. As he thought about these things, and the stories he had heard at the fires, often told from the picture histories of the people, his heart grew large within him and he was saddened that there were no honorable scars of tests and vows fulfilled upon him. He had none at all to count except those inside his wrists, the silly burns from the sunflower-seed testing as a boy, the seeds set there while afire, the wrists held without shake or quiver until the burning cooled. He had no great twisted knottings from the sun-dance thongs on his breast, no scars from dangerous woundings received while defending the people. There was the twisted place behind his knee, the memory of a foolishness, and not to be noticed unless he painted it bright red and so made it a joke. He even lacked the swollen eyelids of the four days of dancing he had vowed, the four days with his face to the sun denied him.

In this excitement, this meeting of the new ones, Blue Dawn and her friend Shying Leaf had little time for the youths from their own village. Even Deer Foot was standing at the lodge of a Two Kettle maiden, one that had been around the Missouri River trading posts and spoke more boldly than his own Oglalas. Lance went with Cedar several times to other bands but mostly he drew pictures of the great pomp of the headmen, in full regalia, marching in long ceremonial lines from all the divisions and bands to the council lodge at the same time, meeting there like the colored petals of the sunflower meet at the brown center where the seed was made. So the seeds for the future of the Sioux nation were to be made here.

Lance and the others enjoyed the little Ree's astonishment that there were so many people on the earth, and without any of his tribe, which he saw now was very few. Lance was not so certain that there were no Rees around. One or more could easily slip past the scouts and guards who could not know every one of the people here—twenty-thousand people, Frenchy said, by white man figures. If there was a Ree who spoke Sioux, he could surely get in.

Once two formal messengers came with a carved stick for Lance. He looked at it curiously, with its crossed embers and twist of smoke cut into the pale wood.

"It is to guard the fire with the others," one of the men said. When Lance had been through the purifying sweat lodge and was painted by the mentor of the fire keepers, he went with four others up *Mato Paha*—Bear Butte. They climbed the shadowed rocky path to the place between the shoulders, where the blackened earth of the ages of fires looked no blacker than the butte itself. The young Sioux looked back over the great camp of his people, the blue smoke of evening trailing in the shimmering dusty air, mostly straight up, in the sign of changing weather. But for now the evening sun was golden over all the fine, broad valley.

Up on the butte the fire makers kept the vigil, and as

night settled down, the big fires for the dances and the ceremonials flared high in the valley to the east. Lance stood in his place, awed by the vast black figure whose shoulders they rode, much of the dark bulk of the crouching Bear above them. Later he slept, but when the sun neared, it was once more his turn to stand at the fire. He watched the first bright rays shoot from the far horizon, touching the Bear's body and then down on the shoulder and the lowered head, and finally reaching between the shoulders to the mentor and his fire keepers.

The last night the young people came back to their own bands for a little dancing, and the preparations for the morning's move. Blue Dawn once more smiled upon her old friends, but Shying Leaf seemed suddenly to have blossomed into a coyness Lance had never seen in her before, and it was said that the sad flute singing its sorrowful song off on a knoll was for her.

Lance was to stay behind with the small party of Sun Shield. He went with a ceremonial group to the top of the Bear, to the highest point, carrying the pegs with the red and black cloth ribbons for the meditations of the old chief. While Sun Shield prepared himself, stripping off everything not of the old, old days, the others cleared a place of all grass and growth and planted the pegs with the colored streamers around it. Then the old chief stretched himself face down in the center. His lean and scarred old body was naked to the unadorned deerskin breechclout and moccasins. His arms stretched toward that country south and west that he must see how to keep, not only keep in buffaloes for their meat but keep free of the white man and his trails, his whisky and his sicknesses.

When everything was gathered up, Moccasin led all the helpers down, leaving Sun Shield alone with the Powers.

. . .

Down in the wide valley the great circle camp of the Teton Sioux melted away as it had grown. This band moved out and then that one, long strings of people trailing over the far hills until they looked like tiny dark ants running before the winter. Lance stayed with Moccasin and the rest who guarded the only path to the top of Bear Butte, guarded it anxiously, not only against possible enemies come skulking around the encampment for stragglers, but keeping a watchful eye on the old chief. He was much too old for this fasting, this exposure to the broiling heat of noon and the chilling dew of night.

The end of the second day, Moccasin and some others went up to see how it was with the old man. They came back silent, saying only that he had refused the water they brought and that he had not dreamed. The next day it was the same, but after a while they signaled for Lance and the others to bring a robe and carrying sticks. They hurried up and found the old man gaunted so his bones thrust sharp against the skin, the flesh between apparently all gone. Alarmed, they lifted the fragile body carefully to the robe, fastened the carrying sticks to the sides and took him down the steep path to the foot of the butte. There a little soup was forced into the man's clenched mouth, and when he revived a little he wept that they had not let him die.

Lance felt shamed before the man, shamed to see his pitiful condition, and somehow guilty.

8 / Hard Winter and the Moose Yard

LANCE LAY IN THE WICKIUP beside the lodge of Feather Woman. She had made an opening through the skins on the men's side into the low shelter so she could lift her eyes from her work at the fire and see how it was with the fevering one. The time for the fall hunt had come and passed, and yet almost no meat was made. Everywhere people burned with the little spotted disease that the traders called measles, saying it killed only a few of the white-skinned ones because it was always with them. They sickened while small children, when the heating was less dangerous, and so were shielded forever because it was a one-time disease.

Then the sickness came to the village of Sun Shield, where few had ever seen the little spots that struck down the council and almost everyone, even while the people tried to leave it behind. They fled from the first curious, sweetish smell of the sickness, but it traveled with them everywhere, always with them like a second shadow. Every day new bodies had to be tied into the trees or, later, be left where death came, those still able hurrying away faster and faster, with many riding in the sick travois behind. Up at Bow Creek of the Belle Fourche the fall snows found them, and the running had to stop.

It was here that Lance had the dream that none could interpret, or even say if it might not have been a vision. Perhaps when the Sioux came together at Bear Butte next summer they might find a man with the medicine to understand it. In his sickness Lance had seen figures come out of the sky, not falling but floating down to him—men, horses, buffaloes, lodges, whole villages, with all the people coming toward him, finally standing in a row. They had grown no larger as they neared, the tallest man no bigger than the little finger, and only dark lines filled in with color—red and yellow, blue, and some green as grasses in the springtime. All the while they stood in the row there was a burning in the face of Lance, in all of him, as though he sat at one of the great fires the white man builds to warm himself, so hot against his face that he must move far from it and freeze his back.

Slowly, Lance, called Lone Lance more often now, had awakened, returned, but so weak he could scarcely lift his hand to see that it was still there. When he finally became aware of those around him, he discovered that several more had been lost since he fell into the dreaming that even the medicine healer had thought was death.

To the question in his sunken eyes Feather Woman held a spoonful of soup for him, waiting. When it was gone she said: "Your family, they have escaped. Good Axe took them to the relatives on the Tongue, far from the sicknesses of the Platte road."

Lance tried to move his parched lips and Feather held the finger of silence to her mouth. "The twins are all safe."

"The Rees—They are too near to them," he whispered.

The woman bent her head in acknowledgment. It was true.

As Lance strengthened a little he began to form other questions. Moccasin? Yes, he had been struck out on a hunting party and recovered there, with some staying to care for him. Dawn had scarcely been touched, but Shying Leaf was on the scaffold. And Deer Foot.

Only Cedar remained, the tall, thin Cedar, not sickened even one day. "No place for the spots," the youth had said every time he was asked. He said this soberly, his face sharp as a war ax, making the words before others could, particularly the girls, who sometimes called him a lodge pole, "but not so wide—" and laughing, but behind their palms.

The first time Cedar came to see his friend he stooped his height awkwardly over Lance, but none of the proper good words came to his reluctant tongue. Finally he swallowed, reached out a hand and dropped something on Lance's chest, and stumbled out into the winter sun.

Lance lifted his hand to grope about on his shirt and found something small, heavy, irregular in shape. Raising himself up on an elbow, he saw, even in the dim firelight, that it was the little gold stone that was Cedar's favorite possession, a little bean-shaped stone, golden as the white man's money pieces. Cedar had found it in the *Pa Sapa*, the Black Hills, when they hunted there last summer while Lance was tending the fires on Bear Butte. He had showed it to no one but old Sun Shield after they returned, and Lance.

"It is said this gold makes the white man like a starving wolf," Sun Shield had told them. Some white men came to that place about ten winters past and began to dig as fast as badgers for this golden stone. The chief and some other headmen had gone to say this must not be done in their sacred country. The men started shooting, and when two of the Indians fell, the rest chased the whites through the timber and killed them.

Lance had heard the story many times and had tried to

draw the white men running, shooting back, with a chief on the ground, the blood a widening spot, but he could not see it clearly enough to make the picture.

Now a piece of the gold those white men sought lay heavy and smooth in his hand, the gift of a friend, the friend who had escaped the sickness.

Everyone had known that the weather would be cold, the snow deep, with the rabbit's fur already thickening back in the Month of Cherries Black—August—and the silent-winged white owls, seldom seen, were back from the north for a second winter. Lance had seen them early in the fall, sitting high in the trees before the leaves were well yellowed. They blinked in the brooding sun that was soon lost in the early storms, white and silent as the owls at first, until the winds came.

Perhaps the buffaloes also knew about the hard winter ahead. Every tribe complained that the large herds were somehow gone, only a scattered few around, and very wild for the bows of the strongest hunters. By the time the spotted disease had finally crept out of the village of Sun Shield, the snow was very deep and still falling, or whipped along by the strong earth winds that drove the snow sharp as ice against man and animal and tree. Often the sky was clear from the hills, only the earth and the game, the animals, lost in the freezing ground blizzard. Grouse and rabbits and even coyotes dug in behind rocks or bushes. Larger game tried to reach sheltered breaks and canyons, to wait out the storm, perhaps to be covered so deep that even the hungry nose of the wolf could not find them until the buzzards soared in the melting spring sun. Truly the winter was one from which to count time.

At Sun Shield's village the hunters who had strengthened enough pushed out into the earlier sunrise, before the wind rose, hoping to see some far cloud of frozen fog clinging to the horizon where a buffalo herd lived. They went to look and came back with blank faces.

It was poor soup in the kettles this winter, only an occasional rabbit or the meat of a horse grown weak and butchered to keep the starving people alive a while longer. Lance went with Cedar and the others to help the stronger of the women drag home cottonwood branches for the bark that the few horses at the camp could gnaw and be kept from scattering and being lost too.

The first time Lance came out to help Feather Woman she watched him stumble over the drifts in the stinging cold and tried to send him back, but he knew he would gain strength in the open air. It was lucky that he went, for while they dug the young cottonwood from the high drifts the woman fell in sudden weakness. Lance drew her upon his outspread robe and started to drag her home over the stone-hard snow, grateful that others saw and came running to help. At the village he carried this mother who had chosen him as a son into the lodge, suddenly struck how thin and light she was even to his weakness. One of the gathering women ran for the medicine healer, and another sent a scout to signal for Moccasin, out hoping to find a little game. But while the fire rose and the youth tried to rub a warmth into the woman's feet, stony and gray, he heard the breath stop.

Lance helped wrap the winter-gaunted body of Feather Woman into her best robe, with her hair neatly combed for the last time by Moccasin, the many strings of beads laid around her neck, the bracelets put on her arms. Lance went with the bearers over the frozen drifts to a lone cottonwood standing out on a wind-whipped stretch of bottoms. It was a dying old tree, not a good one for the beloved Woman of the Herbs, as Feather was sometimes called, but it was the only one standing high enough above the snow so no wolf could touch her.

The twigs and small branches of the cottonwood broke like ice as the men climbed up with the stiff dark roll and tied it solidly into the highest fork. When they were down out of the tree they hurried away, the mourners back to the keening fire in the village, most of the men to hunt a little ahead of the rising wind. At the lodge, Lance gathered up his bow, arrows, Feather's little belt hatchet, and his worn and well-tallowed winter robe. Back at the old cottonwood he built a little fire with a strip of inside bark and a dead branch—no more than a palmful of coals that would burn down through the snow. He spread his robe, squatted on one end and drew the rest over his hunching back and his head and the fire too, enclosing the heat. When he had thawed the cold from his bones he sent his heart back over all the years that he was part of the lodge circle of the woman now dead in the tree, the one sometimes called Laughing Woman by her closest friends. Because she had lost three children to the big spotted disease—the smallpox of the white man—she had become a healer, and many said her gaiety half cured them before her herbs could be swallowed. She had fed and warmed and comforted Lance from infancy as only a boy's second mother could, and nursed him through this fall's sickness until she was ready for the tree herself. But she had done more, much more. She had taught him to see many things of the hearts around him, and many practical things too, some that she pictured with perhaps her knife or her awl in the dust.

"If you are far away, hurt and bleeding, there is a plant that is good," she said, drawing the long, limber-jointed stalks that grew in marshy places, the leafless plant the white man called mare's-tail, drawing also the variety that had many little stalks bushed out together, truly like the tail of a horse, and just as good for bleeding as the single stalk. "Make a tea, or chew the plant, swallow the juice and spit out the strings," she had told him.

For deep bleeding one put the finger where there was the little kicking deep down, and then tied a rawhide thong around it if possible, with a knot or stone or wood in that kicking place, pressing in hard. Once she dipped a finger into the soft, snowy clay she used to whiten robes and drew the path of the blood down the arms and the legs and up the throat. It was from her that Lance had known what must be done when he got the arrow in his knee and the blood was running away from him.

As his second mother, this woman had welcomed his friends and quieted only their most boisterous noise, laughing a little with them, softly, as was becoming in a woman of the Sioux. She had let him open his heart when it was sorrowful, was joyous when there was joy in him. Now Lance's heart was on the ground and she was not there to lift it, yet a warmth and thankfulness were in him. So long as one person who had known this woman remained on earth, she would be alive.

Before evening the little fire at the burial tree had melted down to the ground. Lance drew the coals off to the side and then farther, thawing a place big enough to crouch in his robe, turned wool side in, on warmed earth. After a while he slept, and in the morning he awoke to the friendly cackle of grouse. Gently he opened his stiffened robe, knowing it would be white with the powdery frost that covered all the snowy valley. He looked up, past the frosted, robe-wrapped figure tied in the branches. On the far tips, against the sky, sat three plump-breasted grouse, silvery as the glistening tree. Lance drew his small bow very slowly and let the arrow go. At the twang of the string the cackles rose in curiosity and astonishment as one of the birds was lifted a little and knocked from her branch by the stick in her breast. As the others flew in noisy alarm, the wounded grouse began to fall, striking a branch here, another there, loosening showers of white frost, the arrow flapping. At the foot of the tree the bird still fluttered a little on the bloody shaft, but Lance crushed the back of the thin skull, bringing instant death, instant quiet.

He skinned the warm grouse and split it to roast faster over the coals. Then he offered the first bit on the point of his knife to the Powers and ate. Afterward, when the last of the sweet, juicy meat was cleaned from the bones, Lance felt stronger than for a long time. He lined his moccasins with the grouse skin, the softer feathers left on, and with his robe about him he started out to find meat for the village, if it could be done. He looked back to the old cottonwood from a high drift, realizing that he was once more running out like a foolish boy, this time a sick one, starting off in the deep snow and stinging cold alone. He knew someone would have come for him long ago if the men weren't sick or searching for meat, some gone for many days, sitting out the blizzards under their robes stretched against a bank or rocky ledge to protect their little fire, letting the storm sweep past. Although today was quieter, the sun was a pale disk of ice behind veiling clouds, a warning to all creatures that more snows were near.

Lance drew out the horse rope always about a young Sioux's waist and tied his old robe securely around him. With his quiver and bow tucked into the belt at his back, he started northwestward, although the meat scouts had been in that direction for much of a moon's time. He moved along the southern slopes, just below the crest of the ridges, where he could dodge to either side if enemies appeared, and where the first wind would cover his lone tracks.

The wind started. Little curls of snow began to run up the slopes. They grew and spread until all the earth was a flow of white, but somehow the ground wind never rose much above the knees. Finally, Lance, stumbling and weary from hours wading against the steady push of air and snow, looked for a sheltering spot with a little wood or even brush, if enough to last him through a storm.

It was strange country to him, flattish and bare of all but snow. Suddenly, almost at his feet, the ground fell away into a deep, narrow canyon with a timber-bordered stream, icebound, but large, surely the Powder River. Lance peered carefully over the edge of the canyon, searching it for smoke, for any sign of an enemy who had sought this good shelter. The snowy valley seemed empty, dead except that five waxwings sat in a clumpy cedar tree scarcely more than an arm's length away. They were gravely passing the blue cedar berries to each other in their curious way, what the old Sioux called "passing the bird pipe." They made a pretty picture on the snow-caked, dark-green tree, the fawn-gray birds handsome with their black crests and white-tipped tails, the wings set off by the red wax ends on the flight feathers. The birds passing the blue berries from beak to beak seemed a good sign, but the wind was rising stronger, and half frozen, Lance searched out a place to get into the deep-cut valley, and slid down the long drifts on his seat, the wind cutting his face.

In a frozen side-marsh the tip of a muskrat house stuck out of the snow. Although it was hard as stone with winter, Lance chopped it open and then watched patiently until he managed to get an arrow into an old muskrat, with angry, bristling whiskers, come up to inspect the damage. It was nearing dark and with the northwest wind to carry any smoke out over the high empty plain he had just crossed, he dared make a little fire. He dug a hole back under a ledge that was covered entirely by a sweep of tall snowbank. Here, in dry sand, with only a little of the black oily seepage so common along the Powder River bluffs, Lance ate and slept, dry and warm.

The new snow came, light and fine as dust and then the sky cleared. Lance was strengthened by the sweet, dark meat of the muskrats and the roots they had stored for their winter. He wished their skins were tougher, fit for more than warm moccasin lining. He had to keep cutting pieces off his old robe to resole the moccasins, leaving less and less buffalo hide against the cold. He was comfortable under the drift-covered ledge and tried to decide whether he should go back. He could catch the next stiff northwest wind, let it help push him homeward, but his own family was up ahead somewhere, with the Tongue River Oglalas.

That night Lance was awakened by a noise where the only sound had been his breath and heart and an occasional quiet fall of coals in the cooling fire. He sat up in the darkness, listening. The snow drift over him had come alive with little whisperings of water seeping through it. He stuck his head out into the night. A soft warm wind from the northwest blew across the canyon against his face. The first chinook of winter had come.

By morning the river was popping like the white man's pistols as the ice cracked and lifted in great stretches through the snow water that rushed down from the drifted canyon walls. It was time to move, before the river was a roaring flood of broken ice. Hurriedly Lance searched the scattered timber for a long pole. With it he tested out the last river-wide expanse of ice. It was rising through the snow water too, but he stepped out upon it carefully, running as lightly as he could. Still the big floe tilted and broke and separated, the river boiling up dark and freezing under his leaping feet, the pole balanced across his body to keep from being swept under the ice if he missed a jump. He made it across without much soaking above the knees and stopped to dry himself at a hidden bit of fire. He felt happy for the first time in several moons, happy as man is in a victory over a flooding stream.

Lance knew that the chinook wouldn't last, that it would be followed by a swift freeze, the water everywhere turned to stone. He might get back to Sun Shield's village before that, but he had no good news of buffaloes for his hungry people, and his blood family and the little Ree were up north. There had been all the moons of uneasiness about the boy far in the south, with a Ree warrior managing to get clear to the lodge of Good Axe before he was killed. Now the boy was up near the traders who dealt with the Rees, handled their robes, their furs, some of them married to women of the tribe.

By now the drifts were so soft that Lance sank down to his waist. He needed snowshoes. There were plenty of willows along the river for the frames but no rawhide for the criss-cross lacings. Besides, if the weather stayed warm, there would be enemies out in daylight, with scouts looking all around. Lance would have to travel in the dark, the nights probably cold enough to crust the snow. But he had to find game for the trip. The muskrat house was dead now; besides, he would be without the time for such patient waiting. He thought of the *wasna* of other years, but this was the hungry winter, with only the summer's meat, no fall hunt at all. He hoped it was better up north although he had seen no sign of even a lone old buffalo bull anywhere.

By dusk the snow was crusting a little, and Lance started up a canyon that seemed to lead away to the wide western tableland where enemies would probably not be traveling now, or at least moving in large parties that could be careless enough to be seen.

By the time he reached the Medicine Lake region, where many of the great white swans nested in the summer, storm signs were growing fast over the Big Horn Mountains standing across the west. He had seen nothing larger than a hungry wolf, an old one, digging in a beaver house, since he left the cottonwood that bore the dark body of Feather Woman. He hid in a brushy canyon at dawn and slept a while. When he awoke he looked out and saw a line of eight riders, with five or six pack horses and surely scouts out ahead and behind. They were still far off in the northwest, looking like a snow mirage—small figures beyond a shimmering that was like a lake.

Lance ducked back into hiding and tried to calm himself and consider his trail of last night, if the party or their scouts should strike it. A lone Indian afoot was a mighty easy scalp, often some one driven out by his village, some troublemaker whose killing would not even bring an avenging.

The young Sioux knew he had no more time to waste now than a rabbit with a coyote hard on his trail, but the rabbit could double back on his tracks, make a long side-jump and hide to watch his pursuer foolishly running to where the footprints seemed to end. No man could hope to hide a doubling of his moccasin tracks in snow, and Lance decided to swing far out, trying to walk on rock and gravel and hard sod, stooping along out of sight of high points as much as possible. Fortunately, the sun was already down past the shoulder and by camping time the Indians might not have reached his trail. Yet the scouts out ahead could have found it long ago.

Lance moved cautiously and was trying to slip from one brush patch to another when he saw a man riding along the edge of a far ridge. He slid into a plum thicket, letting himself down slowly, to avoid the searching eye of the Indian, the keen sight of the horse, but he had to risk peering out for some clue to the man's tribe. The scout had his robe up over his head and from far off there was no identifying him by hair, dress, horse, or elkhorn saddle.

Even when the ridge was bare again and the earth and sky empty Lance was afraid to move, the wet and cold of the snow-filled thicket unnoticed in the danger. Evening finally came, clouded and dark. Lance started again, traveling as fast as he dared in the broken country, with only a stick held out ahead to avoid plunging over cliffs, anxious to put distance between him and the scouts. He risked walking a little farther in the late dawn, with the speed of lightning for his feet. The air was damp out of the south now, sure to bring more snow, snow, Lance hoped, in time to cover his tracks. Two or three more sleeps would surely bring him to the Oglala camp.

As the first flakes began to fall, the young Sioux turned into the foothills, moving faster on the old drifts, deeper and harder toward the mountains. He crept to a stony ridge to study the canyons ahead. Through the light fall of snow he saw what seemed to be a dark gathering, a little like a packed bunch of buffaloes, very unlikely in such rough country. He slipped up closer and looked down into a narrowish canyon almost filled with snow. At the far end was the dark cluster of animals—a moose yard, the drifts around it deeper than the height of a mounted man. The animals, snow-caked, seemed to be moving, tramping the snow down as fast as it fell, trying to exist somehow on dead leaves and twigs and bark until a thaw, that the towering wall of mountains behind them might shut out until spring.

Lance reached for his knife, and stopped himself. He could run up to the yard, scare the animals out to flounder in the drifts and perhaps cut one throat, at the most two before the rest got away, probably to die in the snow. He wished this were closer to Sun Shield's village, or the northerners, who could probably use a little more meat too. He had never tried to slash the tough throat of a moose with those great fans of horns thrashing around. Or of a bull elk, although even one would be a start toward the elk-tooth dress for his wife someday. For Dawn, surely for Blue Dawn.

Yet he had foolishly left the village this wintertime, when the young warriors were standing thick as timber in their courting robes at the lodge of the girl, and the one called Lance not there. Still, the little Ree was up north, and very close to the enemy tribe.

Once more Lance was wavering like the spring wind, as both Good Axe and Feather Woman would have told him. In the meantime the snow thickened and the wind was rising. Away from the protecting canyons and foothills, out on the plain that the northerners would have to cross to get here, the storm would be blizzard-sharp and very dangerous. And no telling how long it would last. Perhaps Lance should get the meat that he could from the moose yard, perhaps a bull moose. The big skin would be fine for the picture story of his people, and the meat would last a long time, the rest of the winter if he was trapped here by snow or enemies.

With his robe tied into a pine, safely out of the way, and with both hands free and his knife out, Lance slipped around to approach the yard with the storm, so thick he could hardly see the moving animals. There seemed to be two moose, with their palmed horns rising like trees over their heads, several bull elk and cows, some deer and no telling what else ready for the knife of the hungry.

Lance moved the hatchet in his belt around for his hand, crept out to the edge of the moose yard and then leaped into the air, whooping. The animals stopped their measured walk, caught the man-smell and bolted away, piling upon each other and surging out into the deep snow. The biggest moose was bucking the drifts that reached above his shoulders, plunging deeper and deeper in his panic. Lance ran up alongside, trying to dodge the great horns flung in every direction in the bull's desperate fight to escape the snow, but he couldn't get to the throat. Jerking out the hatchet, the young Indian struck one powerful blow into the neck just ahead of the shoulders. The blade sank deep into the bone, blood flowed, the head stopped, the horns dropping forward, although the legs still worked below. Lance flung himself at the throat with his knife, hacked at the hide that was tough as shield leather. Then a gushing of blood welled out upon him, and over the white drifts.

Lance fell back, rolled himself on the snow and sat up, having to see the great animal motionless, dead, sorrowing in his heart that this had to be done. Then he started the skinning, working fast before the hide froze. He dug down to get at the legs and belly to start properly. It was hard work for one from a recent sickness, and once he stopped to go back to the moose yard. There was one animal left there, a young elk with a broken leg, snow gathering upon his motionless body. Lance cut the throat and watched the pain and helpless terror melt from the soft eye. Then he saw something else, a mule, too wise to leave the yard, a mule pale as morning mist under the wet caking of snow, the hair grayed a little at the head and ears. The animal looked thin and weak, with worn cinch marks showing that he must have strayed from some emigrant on the Platte Trail, perhaps by way of a chief's herd—mules often the most cherished mounts of the women. He let the stranger's hand stroke his nose and tie him to a tree at the moose yard. In the morning Lance would search out some windswept knob and cut grass for this Gray One, as the mule would be called.

It was almost dark by the time the moose was skinned. Wet and freezing, Lance dragged the hide to a clump of trees, tied the middle up between two trunks and then pulled the sides out as far as they reached and weighed them down with snow. Pine boughs cut to fill in the ends completed the warm shelter. Now Lance built a little fire of aspen, almost smokeless, to dry himself and roast some of the tender elk meat. While he ate he wondered about the other animals from the yard, trapped out in the deep drifts, and hoped that they would work their way back, or to some other shelter together. He wished he had a dry skin to draw the picture of the crowded yard, the brave creatures walking, their horns like wavering treetops in the falling snow.

Three days later the storm cleared in the night. The crackling of the cold woke Lance and he knew that it was time to move. He folded the half-dry moose hide of his shelter and hoped that the mule would be strong enough to carry it, and a little meat. He had cut robesful of grass for the Gray One and watched him clean up the last frosted blade. But all the days in the moose yard had gaunted the mule almost to starvation.

Lance started out in the bitter cold of dawn leading the mule, keeping to the higher, barer ridges as much as possible because the small sharp hoofs sometimes broke through the crusted drifts. At sunrise travel seemed too dangerous even with the long ears of the mule alert, and Lance stopped at the first protected spot near a little windswept grass. In the evening he started again and three days later he saw the daybreak smoke of a village from far off. He hid until the night fires were a glow on the sky. Then he moved closer, and with his head against a frozen tree trunk, managed to pick up the beat of a drum and, farther on, the rise and fall of singing voices. In his excitement he lost all caution and from a snow-piled rocky bluff he gave the owl hoot of the Good Axe family through his cupped hands.

For a long time there was silence, so long that Lance was certain he had betrayed himself to enemies probably encircling him even now. Then a fire arrow rose from the village, and two more, one straight up, the other across it—the sign for cutting off the top, the head—the sign of the Sioux. But now Lance had to be sure. He repeated the owl hoot and then slipped off to the side, watching. Men seemed to be coming over the star-lit snow, many of them, calling out: "Oglala! Oglala!", others shouting out their familiar warrior names.

That night there was a feast in the lodge of Good Axe, with Lance in his place at the left of his father, the little Ree and Cub beside him while across the coals were the firelighted faces of Cloud Woman, his blood mother, and the twin sisters, all safe and well.

"It pleases your relatives to see that you are strong again," Good Axe said in the old formal way.

Lance thanked him and had to add that Feather Woman was carried to the tree. The mother made a little keening sound, and the father guttered his pipe. "The hunters saw some signals," the Axe said after a silence. "They told that you were gone. It seemed like you, but dangerous."

Lance looked into the fire, ashamed. The little Ree leaned against him to whisper, "We knew you would fight everything."

Lance smiled down upon the two boys beside him, into the faces that were round with pride.

The big thaw up north brought a good herd of buffaloes. In the hunt Lance got three more—six buffaloes in two hunts, something few older hunters equaled. By the time the parfleches were full, the moose hide tanned by Cloud Woman for the picture history, and the mule rounded out and strong, there was disturbing news from the trader house on the Yellowstone. The Rees were coming for their son, not with arrows and guns but with gifts to buy the boy from his captors.

"One does not sell a brother," Lance said quietly.

"But he is the son of the young chief killed in the fight."

"He is the twin of my brother now," Lance replied stubbornly.

But there would be pressures on the Oglalas up here from

their trader, so the Good Axe family started home, with a party of the young northern warriors along for a visit, and for protection against the Crows, who had been traveling the region all winter. True, the Rees would not give up, but it would be better down in the south country.

On the Belle Fourche, scouts signaled the Good Axe return and took the extra horses to the grazing herds. Many came out of the village to make the welcoming, led by Moccasin, happy to greet his friend, and the youth who had found a warm second home at his fire from the cradleboard time. There was a new mother for him, the handsome Sage, younger sister of their beloved Feather Woman.

Lance knew her, a good second relative who had lost her husband and one of her small sons to the sickness of last fall. Sage came forward now. "We welcome you to your old place," she said gently, "our son who is now a man."

A man—the words said as for one who had proved himself. And yet Lance doubted.

The maidens of the village had come out to sing the welcome for Good Axe, who had borne the holy lance, and to see the young warriors from the north. Dawn was among them, almost as shy as ever, it seemed, as she greeted Lance with lowered eyes and walked back to the village beside him.

That evening he helped take the family travois horses out to the herds. On the way back he stopped at the water path, where the red-winged blackbirds were singing and the violets blued the shorter grass. Dawn stopped to ask how it had been with him, and to admire his new height. Lance followed her going with his eyes, seeing a new grace in her walk, a new womanliness with the waterskin. He had asked about Cedar and was told that he was over at the Brule village, courting. It was very funny, the lean and wooden-tongued Cedar courting.

But in the wickiup at night Lance thought about this,

and about Dawn as he fell into a troubled, uneasy sleep. He awoke with a yearning, deep and sad, and heard the far crying of a reed flute on a hillside somewhere. It seemed to be his cry, still in the dream. The flute might be for Dawn, from one of the young warriors who had waited at her lodge door every evening. Angrily Lance drew his robe about him and determined to sleep.

The second night there were songs and dances for the warriors from the north. In the midst of the fun a shouting arose and two riders were hurried into the lodge circle. It was Cedar, and behind him a young woman, with her hair neat and her cheeks painted in the way a fond husband would.

"My wife," Cedar said, with some of the old reluctance still on his tongue but with a new pride that Lance had never seen in his friend.

"He had to get a girl from the Brules, where they don't know him," Jumping Moose teased, perhaps because Cedar and Lance had been boys with his scouts less than two years ago.

During the evening Dawn danced mostly with the northern guests and some of the village warriors but several times she drew Lance into the running circle. After a while he slipped away, to get the little gold nugget Cedar had given to him in his sickness, and hang it diffidently about the neck of his friend's pretty wife. Afterward Lance went out into the darkness to throw himself upon the warm spring earth, to cling to it, hoping to still the turbulence in him, a turbulence like a sudden storm in a canyon.

He was back before the dancers scattered. When the old woman of Dawn's lodge started home with her, Lance stepped up formally beside the girl, ahead of the others waiting. Dawn bowed her modest acknowledgment, and with his new northern blanket about her shoulders, he walked beside her, thinking about Cedar and his bride.

"Come stand in my blanket a little while," he begged on the way to the lodge.

The girl lifted her face to look at him in the darkness, the youth gone only a little over three moons, and now suddenly speaking not like the friendly boy of her childhood, but with the urgent determination of a man. She slowed her walk, and the old woman, worn out by the lateness of the dancing, plodded on and stooped under the lodge flap.

"Come see the fine mule I captured for you. Truly pale as fog in the moonlight."

"I cannot—"

"But he is tied behind the family lodge!"

Slowly Dawn went, the young Sioux guiding her, watching the night ground for picket pins, lodge ropes, and meat racks. The mule was not at the lodge of Good Axe but some distance behind it, staked out against a bank at the edge of the village. Lance drew the girl along, barely noticing her reluctance in his eagerness. She did admire the gentle mule, vague but visible in the night, as whitish mules are. She patted his neck while Lance urged her to sit on the bank in his blanket a while.

"Only to the first star's fall—" he begged, and when she sat beside him, her arms folded in her lap, his blanket about her shoulder, Lance forgot his promise.

"Come with me tonight," he whispered.

The girl didn't seem to hear. She was watching the darkening of the fire glow in one lodge after another around the village circle, and the wavering patterns of light of the fireflies along the river bottom beyond.

"Come," Lance whispered.

The rising urgency in his voice made the girl draw away, without seeming to move. She did not answer, but plainly she could not do this, not the daughter of a good family, not when she had been the maiden of the sun dance.

Knowing she did not need these words, Lance tried to

remind her that sometimes young women did slip away with their courters, and when they returned there was no trouble, just a quiet setting up of a lodge for them.

"I cannot shame my people so," the girl said, speaking very low, perhaps so no one would hear, discover that they were out, with the old woman of the lodge nowhere around.

Lance looked at the girl in the darkness, avoiding her words, making himself wonder what she meant. Was it that he had too little to offer in horses and coups, in war honors? Or did she dislike him?

In his uncertainty, his embarrassment, he let her slip away toward her darkened lodge, watching until she was safely inside. Then he went up into the bluffs, to sit a long time, bowed and mournful as a spring dove without his mate, wishing he had a skin to picture himself so mournful.

Perhaps he would never marry, be like the one called Lone Man for short, meaning Man Who Lives Alone, a strong leader of warriors in his youth, a maker of shields that turned the sharpest arrow and spear and lead ball. There were some who said he had this great medicine because he had never been with a woman, that all his heart and his power were dedicated to protecting the men who fought for the people.

It was a sorrowful thought, and slowly a mournful little song grew on the lips of the young Sioux. He sang it, but so low that a rabbit hopped out to feed nearby and scarcely looked in the direction of the singer in the late rise of the moon.

After a while Lance realized that he was not mournful anymore but was singing a different song:

> "Come, little Rabbit brother, eat at my feet,
> I will not reach out my hand.
> I will not harm you, little brother of the
> trusting eyes."

9 / A Fight and a Decision

AT DAYLIGHT LANCE WENT UP to help around the horse herds. He was glad to be away from the village, and from the eyes of Dawn and the old woman of her lodge. He wanted to offer his handsome mule to the girl as a gift of apology, an apology for his impulsiveness of last night. His face burned at the thought of the humiliation he would have brought upon her, her parents, and her grandfather, old Sun Shield—upon his own people too, particularly Good Axe, the honored bearer of the holy lance, and his mother and his sisters. Then there was Moccasin and the remembered Feather Woman, now tied in the tree. But most of all he would have brought humiliation and a bad face upon the one for whom he should wish every joy and pride and brightest honor.

Only the maiden's soft protest, *I cannot shame my people so*, had saved them.

Now he saw that it was enough. Never, he vowed, would he act without thought again. Then he caught himself. He already had one impulsive vow unfulfilled, and no telling how much of the hard times past were brought by this, for everyone can suffer for a brother's wrongdoing.

That evening Lance waited at his home fire until Good Axe returned from the council. Later the two sat a while with Moccasin. In the morning the men, with Lance between them, went slowly to the lodge of old Paint Maker. They exchanged greetings with the old band historian and then left Lance alone at the man's fire.

The young Sioux was embarrassed as the presumption of his plans suddenly struck him, but now he had to speak. "Uncle," he said, respectfully, "it seems that I see all things as in pictures, everything put down."

"Making pictures is the right of anybody," the old man replied.

Lance hesitated. "I make pictures of what is happening to all the people, sometimes."

Paint Maker drew thoughtfully at his long pipe, his old cheeks sinking in. "That is also your right, for yourself—"

Lance wanted to stop, leave the old man in peace at his dead fire, but he made himself stay. "It is hoped that I can learn to see what is done as from a high hill"—he lifted his eyes to the man's face, and added, very fast—"as from a high hill and perhaps as from today to the tomorrow."

Paint Maker laid his pipe aside. "This is not for one who was not given the dreaming and the wisdom."

"I have the dreaming, you will remember—in my fasting and in the spotted disease. All things came as from far off to stand in colored figures around me, small as the little finger and thin as paint on the skins."

"That may be the dreaming, but the wisdom?"

All Lance could do was back out of the lodge and stumble away. That evening he brought the gentle mare he had promised Paint Maker's wife for the skins she gave him, long ago. He tied the rope to her lodge and went away.

Two days later the crier came. The man of the pictures

would see those his young friend had made. Hurriedly Lance selected enough for a properly modest roll and found Paint Maker combing his thin gray hair out in the sun. When the braids were wrapped neatly in strips of otter fur, the old man took the roll, looked at one skin of pictures after another, studying some, turning them this way and that, holding them off between his outstretched hands, his withered brown lips pursed.

"A recorder of what has been done is equal to the greatest hunter, the bravest warrior, or even the holy man," he said. "To be such a historian, such a recorder, you must learn to see all things, know how they look, and how they are done. You must see that the young colt swims on the downstream side of the mother, behind the wall of her body, and that the wind does not always push the arrows of the just. As the hills of one's youth are all mountains, and the hunts all seem fat after the meat is long eaten, so memory makes every man the bravest in his long-ago encounters, and the enemies faced in battle become very many as the warrior days retreat. The picture is the rope that ties memory solidly to the stake of truth."

The words made Lance ashamed of the skins the man was examining in the enemy brightness of the spring sunlight, embarrassed that the pictures were suddenly so strange and awkward and unfinished, the charcoal and paint standing away from the alien skins, with little of the movement that Sioux pictures should have: the people dancing, the horses in swift flight, the birds soaring, the very rock alive.

It was about this that Paint Maker spoke, with the picture of Crow Butte in his hands. "A true rock is stony to the eye, a part of all the rock of the earth," he said, and threw the skin aside, to roll upon itself, hastily.

Lance made himself reach for the picture and lay it on top of the others. Slowly he rolled them all together and tied the string securely. Then he rose, murmured the thanks he owed the man and walked quietly to his home lodge. He remembered another time, long ago, when Paint Maker threw one of his pictures aside. Lance had grabbed it up then and fled, running hard over the prairie until the breath cut his breast and a cramp like a knife-thrust struck his left side, made him stop, bend upon it. Slowly he stooped over the pain and lifted pebbles in the sacred number of four, replacing them in their earth nest. Then he flung himself face down on the gravel, digging his fingers into it. Today he walked calmly away, placed the roll of pictures behind his seat at the home fire, and went out to the scouts. He would learn to make the rock live, and perhaps Paint's wife would show him how to prepare the tanned moose skin for the pictures of his people, pictures only for himself if it must be so.

There was a constant little warring with the Pawnees, the Shaved Heads, as they were called, and an occasional real pipe-carrying attack on them by a powerful war party. The fighting started back when the Sioux were first pushed westward by the hungry eastern tribes. Lance liked to hear the ancient ones tell the stories of those times from the faded and crumbling old hide pictures that showed the early hunters going out to the buffalo country afoot, dressed in skins, the men ready for game or defense with their bows and stone-pointed arrows in their hands, the women carrying bundles or babies and managing the big dogs that had rolls of shelter hides on their backs or loaded on stick drags. The dried meat and robes were taken back to the far villages the same way.

Then the horse came, and iron for knives and arrow points. More and more Teton Sioux reached the Missouri, and although the river tribes, like the Ree, tried to drive them back, they crossed to the western plains, some to the

Platte and the Pawnee country. Since then there was much raiding back and forth, against the horse herds, the robe and fur stores of the Sioux, the horses and corn patches of the Pawnees. Both tribes sent out some large war parties, the Sioux usually two a year, planning to strike while the Pawnees were on their big buffalo hunts, their earth house villages practically deserted of fighting men. The fall raids were for the ripened corn as well as for the fine Pawnee horse herds. In the spring often the best mares with colts too young for the long travel were left behind. Besides, there was always fine booty for the more daring in the villages very close to the white man and his goods. They had good guns, dangerous in the hands of those who stayed behind, even though these men were usually old or crippled or in some sickness, but fine guns to capture.

Little Thunder, a chief of the Brules, the relatives of Good Axe, had lost five brothers to the Pawnees. Now the time of mourning was past and the pipe bearers came to the Oglalas for help in a great avenging. This was the first large war party organized since Lance's knee was healed. He came in from a hunt just as the people gathered in the village circle to see the Oglalas accept the war pipe. All the maidens were in a line watching the young warriors step forward. Long Wolf, the war chief of the Brule party, saw Lance and motioned to him and he could not refuse to fill the empty place, not with the eyes of Dawn upon him.

"You will watch the little Ree," he said to them all.

While the pipe was carried on to other bands of Brules and Oglalas, Lance went home with Cedar and his new wife. He took the fastest horse of the family herd, a clay-colored gelding, hoping that speed might save him in the coming fight. There were ten days before the war party was to start, and with a bright moon coming, the young warriors who were to stay behind to guard the Brule village headed down to the wild horse plains of the South Platte River.

Because some of his cousins were going, Lance was asked along. They loaned him two more strong horses for the chase and started. At the river the scouts signaled good herds of mustangs off southwest. From a ridge the horse catchers looked over a broad prairie where little bunches of the wild horses grazed, some so far off they looked like ants around crumbs of brown sugar.

The leader of the party knew mustang ways and also the streams and water holes of the region. He scattered his men far out around the prairie, with extra horses handy, and made ready to start the herds running. He motioned Lance around to the left side to hold all that tried to break off in that natural direction because the left foot in most men and animals takes a shorter step than the right.

"You have a fast horse," the leader told Lance. "They will circle back in about seven or eight miles, as the white man calls it. That is the habit of the mustang."

Lance made the *hou* of understanding and jumped on the long-legged clay gelding that liked to pull at the jaw rope all day, wanting to run. At the whooping of the Indians, the little bunches of mustangs started off like leaves struck by a wind, coming together in their alarm and then running in a stampede. When some started to slow down and stop, they were whooped along with flapping robes, none allowed to crop a mouthful of grass or stick a nose into a water hole. Before the sun had climbed above the shoulder the mares heavy with foal and those with very young colts were falling behind. The best of these were lassoed, tied with walking hobbles and left to be picked up by the herd men.

As the horses of the Indians tired, the riders changed to the fresh ones planted ahead. Men worn out stopped to eat and sleep while others rode their places. Without rest or feed or water, the herds were kept going through the moon-lit night together, and into the next day's sun. By then the lead mares had circled back to their accustomed range many times and the men of yesterday's run took over on horses that had fed and rested.

Two of the wilier lead mares had got away, slipped into shadowed gullies in the bright moonlight. More and more of the horses left were giving out now, perhaps to fall flat or to stop, standing in swaying exhaustion, head, mane, and fine long tail drooping toward the earth until they folded their legs and went down. There was bad luck the second night—a storm rose to cover the moon and in its darkness the last five left got away, the five strongest, toughest.

After the pursuers slept a while, they brought the horses together, eighty head, including the larger stallions, easy to wear out. The men herded them all into a box canyon, well-watered and with enough good grass for two, three days, and easy to hold. There the horse handlers caught the lead mares and side-hobbled them—a hind foot tied to the fore one on the same side, the strip of rawhide long enough to permit easy movement at a moderate pace but short enough to bring a tumbling fall in a long-strided run.

Lance had skinned one of the dead stallions the first night and stretched part of the hide on a circle of willow shoot to dry for some pictures of the mustang hunt. On this he made sketches of the wild horses running together like dancers when the riders charged out of the canyons to keep them moving, and their swift plunges and turns, their manes and tails flying out like smoke. For the laggards that were overtaken he had made the eyes round, empty circles in fury and alarm, with foam flying from the mouths as they tried to run again before the whooping chasers shaking robes on the wind—to run or go down.

The Indians started the horses home in two bunches for easier grazing and only brought them together for the night guarding against any skulking parties of Pawnees, Crows, or Kiowas. Up toward the Cheyenne River one of the scouts signaled that two riders were seen hurrying through the canyons and breaks, riders trying to keep hidden. They might be Crow scouts for a large party, or Pawnees, or even Rees coming down. The leaders ordered the herd thrown together in a narrow canyon and sent out three men with fast horses and scouting eyes. Lance was proud to be the leader. When the riders detected a scout they whipped their horses as though trying to get away, sometimes a trick to lead an enemy into overeagerness and an ambush.

Lance, in country he knew very well, pushed ahead to a draw that the two must pass. There he saw that it was Standing Eagle, a Sioux warrior, with Yellow Bead, a Brule daughter given to a trader by her father when she was a maiden, although she had wanted to marry Eagle. She had borne the white man two children, who were sent away to the French wife down the Platte to be reared as white. Now, with her duty to her husband done, as an Indian woman she was free to go, but the trader was sending men to bring her back. Standing Eagle was pleased to have the protection of the horse catchers. He and Yellow Bead rode with the herd but saw only each other, like any youth and maiden in the springtime.

"They have waited seven years," the leaders said, to excuse the unseemly show of affection before others.

Lance could hardly watch the horses because it was so fine to see these two together. This was how it would be with him and Dawn, but without waiting seven years. He wished the horsehide were unpacked and that he had time to draw the picture of the two, perhaps the woman seated at the morning fire, leaning forward, Eagle combing her hair.

At the Brule village Lance could scarcely hold himself from taking the two horses he got from the mustang herds and hurrying home. He wanted to offer everything to the lodge of Blue Dawn, to ride with her as Standing Eagle rode with Yellow Bead, and his own friend Cedar with his pretty wife.

But now the warriors from the other villages were gathered for the avenging on the Pawnees, and Lance had promised to go. On the three-day ride toward the Platte country he heard why the pipe-carrying for war was done so quickly. It seemed that the white men were telling the Pawnees, "Get back from the Platte, away from the settlers and the Platte trail," but not so far as they ordered the Sioux, not to the Tongue. The Pawnees were letting themselves and their earthen villages, their cornfields, be pushed up to the Loup River, closer for the Sioux raiders, but much too close to the best of the shrinking Sioux buffalo grounds.

"We must strike them before they take root at our meat racks," Long Wolf had told the warriors in his harangue before the war dancing started. "We will help avenge the five brothers of Little Thunder left dead on the ground; we will help scatter the Pawnees like leaves in a whirlwind from our buffaloes."

Lance was sent out with the Jumping Moose scouts quietly in the night, far ahead of the war party, which would leave in proper paint and feathers and shining spears, all very fine to see as they were sung out upon the prairie by the women. Afterward the shields and regalias would be packed away until the triumphant return if they didn't have to slip home in dark defeat. Lance thought about the ceremonial departure and almost wished he had been asked to go as a warrior, as Hawk and Willow Hoop and others were, most of them younger than he, and with fewer honors. But they were always warriors, not divided among many things as he was, not cut in pieces.

When the scouts neared the Pawnee country they slept in gullies and washouts during the day and traveled by dark. Lance had been in raids on horse herds and hunting camps down this far but never on an attack on villages of earth.

He had heard many stories about the Pawnees as a people from Loup Man, who liked to talk about his youth and his coming to the Sioux.

"I was running through the grass, carrying my little brother, when Sun Shield reached down from his war horse and pulled the boy from my arms," he said. So he had to follow the small one into captivity. The boy sickened and died up near Bear Butte, and Loup Man could have escaped, but he stayed to be near the bones of the little brother and because he had married a Sioux maiden and so was one of her people. No one expected him to go on the raids against the Pawnees, not against the people of his mother, but he had become a very hard fighter against the Crows.

Lance and the young Brule called Swan, nephew of Little Thunder, whispered about these things while they lay hidden in the hot morning shade of a brush patch until Jumping Moose commanded them to silence and sleep.

Although no Pawnee scouts had been located, surely someone must have been out from the village to watch, perhaps even saw the two young Sioux crawl up a brushy cut to look off into the Loup River valley. The evening shadows were coming out of the far canyons but the new village place below them was still in golden sunlight—a cluster of about sixty fresh earthen houses looking like the caves that children make by packing moist sand over a fist and forearm and then withdrawing the hand. There were few people out and few evening fires to curl their smoke up into the sky. The brush corrals among the lodges seemed full of horses, surely the fine Pawnee horses, and in the lodges there would be all the valuable goods from the white man.

Lance risked staying at the ridge alone to watch while the young Brule slipped back to the meeting place with the news for Long Wolf and his three hundred warriors scattered in break and canyons so no skulking Pawnee could guess their number. Because Lance had good creeping medicine, and had lived to return from captivity, he was sent to search out the number of warriors in the village, and to locate the head chief's house and the best horses, sure to be nearby. It was hard, but before morning he was back. With Long Wolf's hand on his finger in the black night, Lance drew the village outlines in the dust.

"It is good," the war chief said. "Return to your watching."

At dawn Lance saw the first charge spill down a rise overlooking the new village, the Sioux warriors flowing like a silent wave out of the gray. At a far shouting and cry among the earth houses, the Sioux broke into war whoops. Dogs ran and barked in the village, horses ran circling inside of the corrals. Men appeared to stare a moment, and then vanished for their weapons, perhaps their war medicine.

On the bottoms several warriors left the charging line to pursue a lone man afoot, coming from the river with a gun in his hand. As the arrows struck around him he dropped the ducks he held and pointed his gun at the warriors—two good barrels, probably well loaded. But he did not shoot, just kept retreating in a kind of zigzag dance step that was hard to hit without getting in range of the shots he seemed to be saving for certain kills.

"It is Middle Chief, the head man!" Long Wolf signaled from far off.

The warriors hesitated. It would be a great coup to strike him with a bow or coup stick, but somebody would surely be killed. And if they brought this big man down, the Pawnees would have to retaliate on someone as big—a head chief too, and start years of bloody extermination on both sides.

By now a party of Pawnees was whipping out to rescue

their chief. Most of the Sioux after him turned their horses back to the main attack on the village where all the plunder would be, but Swan recalled his five uncles dead, and leaving his scouting place, whooped out to swing his long-handled war club against Middle Chief.

The first charge upon the village brought down several Pawnees, struck a Sioux from his horse, to be carried away, and swept off a herd of young horses that broke from their brush corral in the turmoil and yells. Several of the Sioux rode hard after them, to turn them over to the horseholders on the ridge. By now Long Wolf had stopped on some higher ground and with five or six head warriors was directing the attacks, guided by the mirror flashes Lance sent from his little knoll. Several times shots came from the village, spurting sand into the face of the watcher peering through the weeds so close, but he refused to be drawn back, even when Long Wolf thought it was too dangerous.

The next charge went with fire sticks and pouches of smoldering moss and rotten wood to be tossed into wood piles and down the smoke holes of the houses, perhaps to fall among the bedding there, and the woven grass partitions or on the feathered shields and finery. The Pawnees hurried to stamp out the fires, but black smoke began to roll up here and there, flames bursting out as the Sioux whooped through the village, swinging their war clubs and thrusting lances everywhere, driving the women and children before them, crying, running for the chief's house, a large earthen dome near the center of the village. Here the few Pawnee warriors made a stand while the Sioux charged the corrals, flapping their robes in the faces of the terrified horses, stinging them with light arrow shots. Frantic, the animals surged against the corral fences and brought some of them crashing down, stampeding over anything in their way, over dog or child or grown man, many to be rounded up by the Sioux horse gatherers. Even Lance got three from his watching place on his knoll, between his mirror signals to the headmen on the rise.

By now the fighting in the smoke-filled village was mostly man to man, a Pawnee going down under a spear or war club, a Sioux jerked from his horse as he tore past some doorway, as Cedar was, and rescued by the next warrior reaching out a hand to help him leap on behind, even though their horse was shot and dropped just outside of the village.

Smoke signals for help went up from the village and off on the south hills by some who had escaped at the first charge. Long Wolf on the ridge sent out scouts to report any large body of warriors coming from the old villages on the Platte, to help their relatives, to protect their families already moved to the new place. Warriors would surely come swarming in, particularly from the fierce-fighting Skidi band farther west. It would be good to hurry.

But although there were many corrals empty and lodges burning, a shift of wind showed Lance that the thick-walled chief's house still stood, with blue puffs of gunfire spurting from the sides where holes had been cut. The finest horses, the best breeding stock of the village, were under the protection of the guns, and the houses of the richest Pawnees too. In their eagerness to get at these, Sioux warriors began to charge boldly almost into the muzzles of the guns. Several were brought down here, badly wounded or killed, to be picked up and carried away in the Sioux custom of letting no warrior or his body fall into the hands of an enemy if it could be helped.

The Sioux had hunted through most of the houses still whole, their arms filled with plunder. More than half of the earthen domes were broken, burnt or blazing, the smoke and stink of skins and dried meat and perhaps bodies too, burning and horrible to the eyes and the nose. Signals came that a party of warriors was on the way from the Platte villages, yet only a few from the Skidi, the largest Pawnee division but farther west, nearest to the Sioux country of the upper Platte. They stayed home, throwing up earth fortifications, expecting attack next.

By now the only resistance was at the large chief's house. It seemed that about sixty Pawnees, women, children, and men, were dead. The horse herd on the ridge had grown to several hundred, many very fine American stock. It was a big day, but some Sioux had been hurt too, and lost, and more could die.

"It is enough of avenging," Long Wolf said. "I will have no more of our good men killed."

So the warriors were signaled in. The sun was already past the highest place, and very hot, particularly for the feverish wounded. The excited horses were thirsty too, and hard to hold. Long Wolf led his party northward, strung out over the hills, with men to guard the rear. At a small creek they camped to care for the hurt ones. The men with the captured horses barely let them reach water, and then whipped the herd on as fast as they could go, to give no home-minded mare a chance to slip past and start the whole herd on a stampede back to the Loup country as Frenchy's horses had started home that time from the White Earth River valley.

The party was tired but feeling good, all except those who had lost friends, and even they knew that it is sometimes a warrior's lot to stop an arrow or a lead ball with his heart. Lance should have been happy too. None of his close friends or relatives had been hurt, and several, including Cedar, had killed a man or counted a first-class coup on someone left alive. But Lance, who had not wanted to come and had not been in the fighting village at all, had seen many things he must record, must put down in his pictures of the fighting—things that seemed a shaming.

Lance was left behind with Swan and several other

scouts, to watch for possible pursuit and to signal it by mirror flash of sunlight or fire arrow in the night. He crawled up close, where he saw the fleeing Pawnees throw their dead into the corn-cache pits and into washouts and ravines, the women cutting a little earth down over them with the butcher knives at their belts. Then they gathered up what they could from the houses left standing, piled it on the horses remaining around the chief's place, and followed the travois with the wounded, striking for the river. Although they whipped the old mares along in their hurry, it was dusk when the last of the Pawnees crossed the June depths and fled on for about three miles in the settling darkness, helped along by the small party from the old villages at the Platte. They moved as stealthily as possible in the night, knowing Sioux ears would be listening all the way, but stopping to care for the burned and the wounded at last. Perhaps they trusted to the Indian aversion to fighting when night dews softened the moccasin soles and stretched the bowstring so the arrow would not fly.

As soon as the Pawnees left the village, Lance and the other scouts searched among the burnt and torn houses for any Sioux. Here a wounded dog waited to be killed, there a horse moaned like an injured woman. They found many good horses dead around the big lodge with the gun holes, where the last stand was made. From a wounded Sioux hidden under a fallen earth wall they discovered that Middle Chief, who had stood off those men from the first charge, had died, and a band chief too, enough to avenge the brothers of Little Thunder. Even the interpreter, part white blood, had been killed, and many good Pawnee fighting men. Most of the women and children were saved, many within the chief's strong walls.

Outside of the village, where the fighting had begun, the first Pawnee warrior to fall lay undiscovered or forgotten by his people. Lance saw him when the scouts entered the village and had to turn his eyes away. The man's head and hands had been cut off and his body covered with knife slashes and many, many arrows. It was plain that this was revenge for Pawnee mutilations of Sioux bodies, men and women, in other fights at other places, but Lance would have to look upon this mutilated man a second time, and very closely, when he started to record the story of today on a skin, to stake down the truth as Paint Maker had said. He would have to draw the picture of a headless body, topped only by the sandy patch of blood, dried and brown, with flies crawling on it.

This was what the warrior must do, any warrior—not cut the head off unless it was in avenging, but cut off life.

Lance was invited to go home with the Brules, where he was to be honored for his strong medicine in scouting and the signal watch for their pipe-carrying attack on the Pawnees. He was included in their triumphant return, his first time with a large body of warriors painted in the colors of their victory and dressed in full regalia of feathers and beads and fringe, riding into a village, the women making the trills and songs of praise, the pretty maidens singling out the young visitors, including Lance, who was made doubly welcome. Behind the warriors came the pack horses loaded with Pawnee goods and then the horse herd from the village. Three of the finest were given to Lance because he had caught them as they passed the watching knoll, the most dangerous spot but also the handiest to the escaping horses. Two of Lance's were of some American blood, and were larger and tamer than the Indian stock. The third was a young yellow mare with gleaming mane and tail. She was evidently a pet because she followed Lance around, nuzzling his hand, searching for something, perhaps not only the Pawnee corn but slices of their pumpkins.

Lance was grateful, particularly for the young mare. She

would be a proper offering at the lodge of Blue Dawn in addition to the pale mule if either was ever accepted.

The first days after the return were sacred to the keening and torn garments of the mourners. Later there would be the scalp dance and the recounting of the exploits—the coups and brave deeds, particularly saving the dismounted, carrying away the wounded and the dead. Before this victory dancing, a messenger came riding a sweating horse, and the crier ran for Lance. They found him at the wickiups, painting pictures of the Pawnee attack.

"Good Axe says the Rees have come."

"Fighting?" Lance asked, afraid.

"No, with a pack horse of gifts."

Lance asked Cedar to look after the captured stock and then got on his father's fast clay-colored horse and was home by dark. He was taken straight to the lodge of Sun Shield, where three strangers sat beside the old chief. Lance approached with a coldness like the angry wind within him. Every enemy who comes into a village as a guest must be made one, but plainly it was not always easy.

"Son," the old chief said, "our visitors have come for the little Ree."

"They cannot have him."

One of the men arose. "Beside us here sits the old chief of our tribe. All his daughters were lost to the spotted disease long ago, and the wife of his son also. The son was bringing the boy to live with the old man, when he was killed. We have brought our best gifts for you, and our gratitude that you found him and saved him so well."

"One does not sell a brother."

"We do not offer to buy—for this there is not wealth enough among us. We offer the small thank-you gifts for the great gratitude we feel."

But the young Sioux face was hard as the rock of the mountains against this, and so the old man rose to speak, leaning on a stick to steady his age. "If Good Axe were to lose all of you, and only the Cub lived—"

"The Ree boy would be white bones on the battleground if I had not found him."

"He is of my blood, all that is left to walk on the ground. Take pity on an old man."

Lance looked around the serious faces. He wanted to cry out against these men whose warriors had wounded his knee and put him into the winter hole, killed his people as far back as one could throw the mind, but it was useless. He had to be just.

"Bring the boy," he said hopelessly. "Let him choose."

The little Ree was brought in, awed by the faces of the chiefs. Then he recognized the grandfather and started to reach out, but he remembered the respect due this lodge and looked around in confusion until he saw Lance. With a moan of relief he pushed to the side of his captor, grasped at Lance's arm.

"Do not send me away," he whispered.

Slowly Lance loosened the boy's fingers, pushed him out to stand alone at the fire, in the center of them all. "You are to choose: go with your grandfather or stay with us."

For a moment Lance saw the guarded, fending face of the small boy of the battleground. His lips drew back in a snarl, old and aged with desperate aloneness and cold, anger and pain. "I need no one!" he cried, and slipped between the legs of the men standing at the lodge door and was gone into the night.

The old Ree chief rose to his stick again. "He is truly a grandson for pride," he said. "I cannot make him a captive among us."

When the Ree guests had been escorted from the village with enough warriors to protect them back to their own region, as was proper with visiting enemies, the little Ree came back. His clothing was muddy and soaked, his skin wrinkled from a long, long time in water.

"Where did you hide so none could find you?" the whole Good Axe family wanted to know.

The boy held up the reed he had stuck into the back of his belt. "Under the riverbank, with the hollow stick pushed up to the grass for the breathing," he said.

Cloud Woman hugged him to her, as was proper with a son not of her blood, hugged him in pride not only for the boy himself but for the son who had brought his brother to her lodge.

There was a feast for the loved one returned, and for his twin, the Laughing Cub, and all their friends.

The next day Cedar and several others brought in Lance's new little herd, the two mustangs and the three horses from the Pawnee village, including the gentle yellow mare. Long Wolf had come with them to thank the Oglalas and particularly his uncle, Good Axe. At the feasting, he spoke of the honors that the warriors from Sun Shield's village would receive as soon as the mourning time was over and the victory ceremonials began. But here among them was one who had returned early, who deserved much honor, with his name sung out as a fine scout with powerful seeing medicine, a brave young man whose signals within reach of the Pawnee guns all through the fight had let him and those with him know what was happening in the village. Afterward this one had led the scouts sent out to search the Pawnee houses, a most dangerous work, with possible ambush and death.

"Our cousin Lance, the son of Good Axe, is something very hard to find, as hard to find as the sweet plums in the blizzard moons. He is a watcher, with eyes like the eagle he captured while still a boy. With no hunger for honors and no fear for himself in his heart, he can see all that is done, and now he has started to catch these things in the pictures for those to come after us, when we here are all grass."

Lance had felt a leaping in his breast like that of a little antelope captured in the arms, but in Lance it was joy, surprise and joy, with a burning of shame too, that it did not seem well and completely earned. Then he saw the eyes of Blue Dawn upon him in the firelight, warm and soft as upon a glorious warrior. In his excitement he slipped away to tie his pretty yellow mare at the lodge of the girl, tied in a suitor's offering.

Lance could not sleep that night in his anxiety and hope, listening to every movement at the lodge of Dawn. In the first morning light he looked out, afraid that the mare would still be tied there, rejected, left for him to lead away. But she was gone, taken to the family herd, and he was publicly accepted as a suitor. Now he had the right to present his formal wooing, try to persuade the girl and her family that he would make an acceptable husband. This might take years, as it sometimes did, but in his gratitude Lance turned his eyes to the sky, the earth and the four directions—to the Powers in which all things are brothers.

After the morning fires were ashes and Cub and the little Ree were running over the prairie, the crier brought the sun-dance stick from the leader of this summer's ceremonial, the stick to call Lance to the preparation for the fulfillment of his vow. The young Sioux rubbed a calloused finger over the carved design, caressed the stick with his palm. This was truly a day from which he could count time, and the sun not yet as high as the shoulder.

A singing in the village circle roused him from his thoughts. Good Axe, painted, and in his best whitened robe with the beaded border, was walking behind the crier toward the lodge of Paint Maker. There the old man came stooping out and drew himself up straight, his painted robe held formally about his old body. Together the two men walked slowly and in dignity around the entire village circle, singing over and over:

"Our son who was called Lance,
Like the lance has run after many things,
Become many things, a man of many deeds.

"Now he will be the picture maker of the deeds of the people;
Now he will no longer be called Lance;
Now he is the Story Catcher."

And while the two men made their solemn parading, the trilling of the women rose and fell as they came out and walked behind the men, walked around all the village circle four times, honoring the one they sang.